PRAISE FOR A SWISS AMISH CHRISTMAS

*"**Great story of love and forgiveness.** I so enjoy reading about the Swiss Amish who I had no idea even existed before Ms. Maggard started writing her wonderful books."*

*"I sure do enjoy reading Ms Tattie Maggard's stories, I'm an old softy and I find myself **crying and laughing at the same time**, my wife thinks I've lost it. Just please keep writing."*

CW00954339

A CHRISTMAS COURTSHIP

A SWISS AMISH CHRISTMAS BOOK 2

TATTIE MAGGARD

FIVE PORCHES PRESS

"I charge you, O ye daughters of Jerusalem, by the roes, and by the hinds of the field, that ye stir not up, nor awake my love, till he please."

Song of Solomon 3:5 KJV

CHAPTER 1

*S*he hadn't invited him in.

For three church Sundays in a row, Daniel Shetler had driven Tabitha home late at night in his open buggy. Each time, Tabitha debated within herself if she should. He'd kept her out particularly late tonight, taking her around the dirt roads the long way home, keeping the horse at the pace of a snail.

He was a nice fellow, but, like all the others, nothing special. Tabitha was beginning to wonder if the romantic way she'd meet her future husband was only in her imagination. What would it hurt to invite him in the parlor? Mama had given her the small room on the side of the house for her very own, with the sole purpose of entertaining her suitors.

The parlor would pass to her younger sister, Rosanna, as soon as Tabitha was engaged—as long as Rosanna had first reached sixteen, the first year of *Rumspringa*, when the Swiss Amish youth were allowed to begin courting. As it was, Tabitha wondered if the room would be hers a few years longer.

Wouldn't that anger Rosanna?

At fifteen, the girl thought she knew all there was to know about "snagging a husband," as she'd called it.

Tabitha wished for some of her sister's confidence. At twenty, she'd been trying to find a suitable marriage partner for four years. Her younger sister, Liza, had married last year at eighteen, leaving Tabitha feeling like the old maid of the family.

Daniel stood close to Tabitha next to his buggy. "I had a real nice time tonight, Tabitha. Did you?" His eyes were starting to take on a dreamy look. Tabitha knew what that meant.

She wrapped her arms around herself tightly and grasped for the right words. "I certainly did. Thank you for taking me home. I'd better get inside now." She sneezed. "Wouldn't want to catch a chill."

He leaned forward. "You're right. I bet it's nice and warm inside." His pupils were as big as the moon.

"*Ja,*" she said. "I bet you're ready to get home too, huh?"

"Oh, I'm in no hurry."

Tabitha hid her frustration with a polite smile. Everyone in the settlement had probably heard that her parents had given her the parlor. "Well, I bet your *vater* would be disappointed if you couldn't work tomorrow, on account of staying up too late."

He eyeballed her lips. "I prefer to save tomorrow's worries for tomorrow."

Daniel was a handsome man with sandy-blond hair and blue eyes a girl could get lost in, but he was moving faster than Tabitha was comfortable with. She put her hand on his chest as he leaned in. "I…"

A series of barks broke the hold his eyes had on her.

"What in the—" Daniel jumped back with a whoop. Tabitha watched wide-eyed as he nearly danced a jig in her front yard, his left leg kicking. Then he began to swat at his knee.

"Don't hurt him!" she cried as she recognized the bushy tail peeking below the cuff of his trousers.

"What?" he yelled, still beating and shaking his leg.

Suddenly, the squirrel ran out of his pant-leg and darted toward Tabitha. She caught it with both hands, keeping a firm hold on the ornery critter.

"He's my brother's pet." She held the frightened animal close to her, and stroked his back to calm him.

Daniel bent over, hands on his knees trying to catch his breath. "That's a pet?" By the look in his eyes, one would think she was holding a poisonous snake.

"*Ja*, his name's Chippy. Eli must have forgotten to latch his cage again."

"He gets loose often?" His voice was still a little high-pitched and his breathing labored.

She thought about it for a second and then bobbed her head. "*Ja*."

"I thought squirrels slept in a tree at night."

"Most do, but not Chippy. My brother's spoiled him."

"Most boys have a dog," he said, still giving the squirrel the evil eye.

"Well, we're not exactly the typical family. I'd better get Chippy back to his cage. *Goot nacht*, Daniel."

Daniel nodded and climbed back into his buggy. "*Goot nacht*," he said, his voice still not as deep as it usually was.

Tabitha snickered as she watched him drive away. "Thanks, Chippy, but you're going to get yourself hurt if you keep running up everyone's pant leg." She held him close as she walked over to his cage in the backyard. After locking him in, she turned for the house, mud clinging to her shoes.

It was late November and the recent rains had Swan

Creek starting to overflow its banks. An icy wind curled around her neck.

She loosened the screen on her downstairs bedroom window, her ears burning under her *kapp*. It was embarrassing that *Vater* hadn't given her a house key, but they'd only started locking the doors so *Gruszdawdie* couldn't escape. Before that, they wouldn't dream of it, leaving the house open even when the whole family was away at church. *Vater* always said if someone wanted to steal something they'd do it anyway, and perhaps if they wanted it that badly they had need of it.

Now, *Gruszdawdie* often woke during the night, thinking it was time for him to milk the cows and set out for the barn. Tabitha's family didn't keep milk cows anymore, having converted the old farm into a cabinetry business years ago. *Mueter* and *Vater* feared for him the most during the winter months.

Tabitha pushed open the window and slid the screen inside diagonally. Then she clumsily climbed inside, her head nearly dropping to the hardwood floor of her bedroom before she caught herself with her forearm. The goal was to get safely inside without touching the floor with her muddy shoes until she could pull them off. Barefoot now, she lifted the screen back up to the window to replace it when she saw a strange little light glowing in the distance on top of the house next door.

She poked her head outside to study the light, tension growing in her chest.

Fire!

She dropped the screen with a clank and pulled on her shoes. Climbing back outside with a little jump, she hit the ground hard, causing her to almost lose her footing in the slick mud. She ran to the opposite end of the large two-story farmhouse and banged on the window.

"*Dawdie*, wake up," she screamed. "There's a fire at the Girod's!"

The window slid open. *Dawdie's* face was barely visible a few feet from her. "Tabitha?"

"*Ja, Dawdie.* I think there's a fire at the Girod house. We have to go see!" Tabitha turned and darted away without waiting for her *vater* to answer.

She shot across the long, dark yard, only slowing down to make sure she was careful on the footbridge that crossed the creek. It was the only way to the Girod house unless you wanted to go around the dirt road to access the house by buggy, but that would take a long time.

Time the Girods may not have.

Her chest constricted when she thought of what she might find, making her run even harder.

Memories of visiting with their closest neighbors flooded Tabitha's mind. The children had all grown up together, meeting in the field between the two houses, across the foot-bridge that crossed the creek that divided them. For a while, she'd even courted Isaac, the hazel-eyed boy her own age.

Flames were coming from the corner of the upstairs roof. *Isaac's room.*

She stopped at the door and beat on it, yelling, "Mr. Girod! Mr. Girod!"

When Tabitha didn't hear an answer she opened the door. All was dark in the house but Tabitha knew it well. She stood in the kitchen where last week she and her *mueter* had visited with Mrs. Girod over pumpkin pie. Would they ever have another visit?

"Mrs. Girod! Wake up! Fire!" she shouted. Familiar with the lay of the house, she found the bedroom door on the first floor. It went against everything she was taught was proper, but Tabitha opened the door. "Fire! Fire! Wake up!"

Mrs. Girod was in front of her in a snap, her long brown

hair covering both shoulders. "Are you sure?" she asked, her voice shaky.

"Yes'm, I saw it outside."

"Hannah and Ada," she said under her breath. The light from the lantern in Mr. Girod's hands grew as he approached them, the faint glow revealing the man's long beard and the fact he wore pants but no shirt.

Tabitha didn't wait for his instructions. She felt her way to the stairs and climbed. Faint moonlight from a single upstairs window guided Tabitha to the first door—the girls' room.

"Hannah! Ada!" She yanked off their covers. They sat up immediately. "There's a fire, we have to get you out."

"Mama," they cried. Suddenly Mrs. Girod ran in and they clung to her.

Tabitha dashed to the next room, banging on the door and yelling. "Fire, get out of the house!" She opened the door.

A figure sat up. Tabitha pulled at him. "Hurry, Simon, there's a fire. Where's Joseph?"

"He sleeps with Isaac now," he said in a broken voice as he jumped out of bed.

Tabitha bolted for the next room. The door was open. Mr. Girod stood inside yelling for Isaac and Joseph, the oldest of his children still living at home.

Flames engulfed the room and the heat pushed Tabitha back a step. She lifted her arm over her mouth and hunkered down, trying not to breathe in the smoke. Mr. Girod hurried toward her, carrying Isaac, though his eyes were only half open. Tabitha released the air in her lungs.

Praise God! He's alive!

Mr. Girod set him down in the hallway and hurried back into the room.

Joseph.

The only reason he would have left Isaac would be if

Joseph also couldn't move on his own. She wanted to help the older man but the heat pushed her back.

Tabitha turned to Isaac and pulled at his shirtless arms, his skin hot to the touch, but it was too dark to see if he'd been burned. "Wake up, Isaac!" she said, her throat raw on account of the thick smoke. She couldn't carry him. He was so much taller than she was. Still, she had to try. He let out a moan as she pulled him no more than a foot across the floor.

She coughed, the burning in her lungs almost unbearable. Her mind urged her to run back downstairs into the fresh air outside, but she couldn't leave Isaac. Images of the times they'd spent together flashed through her mind.

A young boy, vibrant and carefree, teasing her in the open field by the footbridge. A hot summer day when they'd splashed in Swan Creek that ran under it.

Tabitha prayed, "God, please help me and give me strength." She pulled once more and stumbled, dropping him again.

"Roy!" A man's voice from the stairs. The glow of a lantern enveloped him.

"*Dawdie*, up here!" she called with a cough. "Isaac is with me, but he won't wake up."

"Get outside, Tabitha," he said forcefully, picking up Isaac's front half. He fumbled with the lantern. Tabitha took it from him and then she lifted Isaac's legs.

"Where's Roy?" *Vater* asked.

"He's getting Joseph. Hurry, *Dawdie*."

Together, they carried Isaac down the steps and laid him at the foot of the stairs on a rug. She watched *Vater* run back upstairs with the lantern. She wasn't far from the outside door and the hardwood floor was smooth and clean. Tabitha grabbed Isaac under his arms and pulled with all her might, dragging him inch by inch across the hardwood, sliding him with help from the rug beneath him.

Soon, Mr. Girod and *Vater* came down the stairs once again, carrying a limp fifteen-year-old Joseph. They took him out the door and returned for Isaac, coughing and sputtering as they went.

Safely outside, Mr. Girod gathered his family and counted them all. He went back inside once more for the family Bible. It was a tense moment waiting for him to make it back out, but soon he reappeared. Mrs. Girod hit his chest angrily as he held her close.

No one went back into the house after that. There was no stopping the fire once it was out of hand and they all knew it. All they could do was watch it burn.

"Mawmie," seven-year-old Hannah said, pulling at her *mueter's* nightgown. "I want to pray but I don't have my *kapp*."

Her sister, Ada, stood next to her. They were both in their nightgowns, their hair hanging down and blowing in the cold wind as did their *mueter's*.

Mrs. Girod glared at her husband, a frown creasing her whole face, apparently still mad that he'd gone back into the house after everyone had made it out. Tabitha took off her wool wrap and placed it around the little girls.

Mr. Girod gathered his daughters and Simon while his two eldest boys lay on the ground beside them. He put one arm over Hannah and Ada's head and placed his other hand on his wife's head, then he told them to pray for Isaac and Joseph and to thank the Lord for bringing them out.

A moment later he released them and said, "I'll get the buggy. We have to get the boys to the doctor." At that point, the two oldest Girod boys were conscious, coughing and sputtering. Joseph rolled over on his side, away from them and Tabitha could hear him retching beyond the light of *Dawdie's* lantern.

"I'm coming with you," Mrs. Girod said to her husband.

He shook his head. *"Nay,* you're not even dressed," he said sharply. "Go with Tabitha and John and take the others with you." Mr. Girod jogged toward the horse stalls, disappearing into the darkness.

Mrs. Girod began to sob softly. She rushed over to Joseph, pushing his hair back from his face. Tabitha approached them.

"I don't feel so good, Mama," Joseph said. Even at fifteen, the boy still needed his *mueter*.

"Mrs. Girod," Tabitha said quickly. "Trade me clothes."

"What?" she said, sounding confused.

"You're my *mueter's* best friend and I know she'd do the same if she were here. Take my clothes and go be with the boys. They need you. I'll take the rest of the children home with me. You'll worry yourself to death if you don't." Tabitha had been around the woman enough to know it was true. She loved her children and hovered over them anytime one was sick.

Mrs. Girod hesitated only a second.

"*Dawdie*, keep the children with you a minute, we'll be right back." Tabitha pointed toward the outhouse. The two women ran for it at the same time. There was a flashlight inside and by the light of it, they quickly began undressing, first a dress for a nightgown, then Tabitha took off her *kapp* and handed her hairpins over one by one as Mrs. Girod placed them in her own hair. When she had the *kapp* on she reached for the outhouse door.

Tabitha said, "Mrs. Girod, take my shoes. You'll need them in town."

The woman stopped and placed a soft hand on Tabitha's cheek. "Call me Frieda. I'm not just a friend of your *mueter* anymore. And it's cold outside. You'll need your shoes." She spoke like Mama. Mama wouldn't have taken her shoes, either, but Tabitha wasn't a little girl anymore. If Frieda really did want to be her friend, instead of just Mama's, she'd take them.

Frieda started for the door once again and Tabitha caught her by the arm. "Some places in town won't even let you in the door without them," Tabitha said. "I can almost see my house from here. I'll be fine. Take them."

They exchanged tense glances. Frieda took the shoes and slipped them on quickly, using the bench to lean on. *"Danki,"* she said, and then out the door she ran, Tabitha right behind. The cool night air whipped around her thin nightgown, her long, blonde hair flowing in the wind.

Tabitha ran to where the boys lay, the cold ground stabbed through the bottoms of her bare feet. The horse and buggy approached as the fire blazed brighter.

"Isaac." She knelt down beside him. "Are you okay?" She crossed her arms in front of her, suddenly self-conscious, talking to him in a borrowed nightgown. It was fortunate Isaac and Joseph both slept in their trousers, but neither one was wearing a shirt. His eyes rolled back and he looked like he might throw up like Joseph had. She swept the hair back from his face.

"Don't touch me," he said, weakly.

She pulled her hand back. "Well, maybe I should have followed your rules and left you inside the house."

"You pulled me out?" he asked, a look of confusion crossing his reddened face.

She hadn't mentioned it to brag, only to make him see how silly he could be sometimes. "I helped. You're awfully heavy." The buggy stopped beside them. "Are you going to be okay?"

"Ja." He coughed. "I think so."

Tabitha stood as Mr. Girod helped Joseph into the buggy. Isaac stood then stumbled. Tabitha caught him around the waist and pushed her shoulder under his armpit until he stood straight. The warmth of his body against hers came as a surprise. It was more intense than anything she'd felt the whole time they'd courted. But then, she'd never gone out courting in her nightgown before.

Mr. Girod took Isaac's other arm and helped him into the buggy.

"Roy," *Vater* said, looking at Tabitha as he spoke, "take my shirt."

Tabitha watched her *vater* take off the shirt and hand it to his closest neighbor and friend. Then she picked up Hannah, who was thankfully small for her age, and began walking toward the house, looking back only once as the buggy drove away, the cold, muddy ground biting at her toes.

Eleven-year-old Simon took his sister Ada by the hand and they followed, *Vater* walking beside them. Tabitha set Hannah down to cross the footbridge. The boards became slick when the temperature dropped to the freezing point.

She told all the children to hold onto the railing as they walked and to go slowly. Not one of them uttered a complaint about the cold or that they'd just lost everything they owned.

Mama was waiting for them in the yard in her nightgown, wrap, and shoes. "Frieda?" she said when she saw Tabitha approaching.

"*Nay*, it's me, Mama." Tabitha coughed, her lungs still burning in the fresh, cool air.

"Is everyone okay?" Mama's voice trembled.

Vater stopped in front of her. "Roy and Frieda took Isaac and Joseph in to be looked at, but I think everyone is going to be okay…thanks to your daughter." *Vater* gave Tabitha a side-hug as soon as Hannah was set down again. "You didn't obey me when I told you to get out." *Vater's* voice was grave. "And I'm glad you didn't. There's a good chance somebody wouldn't have made it out if you had."

Now that the danger had passed, Tabitha burst into tears. Hiding her face in the crook of her elbow, Tabitha couldn't speak, the emotion of the night coming on all at once. *Vater* didn't say anything.

"Well, aren't you all a sight?" Mama said, breaking the tension. "Get in the house, and we'll get you all cleaned up."

Once inside, Mama half filled a small tub with water from the pump and added some hot water from the wood stove to warm it up. Then they took turns washing their frozen muddy feet. Once they'd finished, Mama set up another tub for washing their faces.

Tabitha took the two young girls up to her room and settled them in her own bed, careful not to wake up anyone else in the house. From her window, she watched the blaze grow, consuming a lifetime of memories—some her own. She sat with the girls until they fell asleep and then found an extra blanket and pillow and wandered around for a place to lie down, suddenly feeling worn out.

The parlor seemed to be the only logical place, but the bench was hard, even with all the cushions she'd made for it. She hadn't even bothered to change into her own nightgown. Her lungs felt tight as she laid down, making her cough. She hoped she'd feel better in the morning.

She closed her eyes, thankful that the Lord had seen fit to save them all, but still wrestling with the image of Isaac lying helpless on the floor, reliving the desperate feeling that she wouldn't be able to save him.

CHAPTER 2

A sharp pain in Tabitha's right eye woke her. She stood in the parlor, confused for a moment. Then she looked down and saw the nightgown she was wearing wasn't hers.

So it wasn't a dream.

She coughed, her chest congested and tight. The pressure made the pain in her eye sharper. She held her hand over her eye and opened the door.

Across the long living room sat her whole family at the dining room table with a smaller table pulled up to it to accommodate the extra visitors. All eyes looked her way. The light coming from the windows told her it was way past breakfast.

She started for the stairs, holding her hand over her eye as she went. Just then, Isaac walked into the kitchen. He spied her standing there and she bolted for the stairs, stumbling up them to her room.

"Rosanna, help your sister," Mama said. Tabitha was halfway up the stairs when she heard Rosanna behind her.

"Are you okay, *schweshta?*" Rosanna asked when she entered Tabitha's room, though she didn't sound concerned.

"*Ja*, I just need to get dressed." She felt dizzy, but she wasn't going to tell Rosanna that.

"Are you sure?" Her blue eyes matched Tabitha's, the only difference was an air of self-importance shone in Rosanna's. "You've slept all morning. Dinner's on the table already."

"I'll be down in a minute." She watched Rosanna leave with a shrug, then Tabitha changed her clothes. Squinting, she made her way downstairs to the table.

She sat in her usual seat and waited, puzzled why no one was eating.

As if reading her thoughts, Mama said, "The rest of the Girods just made it back and they're washing up. Are you feeling okay?"

"*Ja,*" she said, unable to hold back a cough.

"You don't sound so good. Maybe we should take you to the doctor, too."

"Who needs a doctor?" Mr. Girod demanded as he walked into the room.

"Tabitha's not feeling well this morning," *Mueter* said.

Frieda entered behind him, looking completely worn out. "She looks pale." She stood behind Tabitha and felt her forehead. "Fern, she's burning up!" she said to Mama.

Mama stood and pressed the back of her hand to Tabitha's forehead. "We're taking you to the doctor," she said.

"*Nay*, Mama, I was getting sick last night at the singing. It's just a cold." She coughed.

Mama let out a breath. "Well, after you eat you can get right back upstairs and into bed."

Given the way Tabitha's head started to spin, it didn't sound like a bad idea.

Everyone sat for the silent prayer. After *Vater* signaled the end with the clearing of his throat, they all began chatting like they always did when they were together. Only Isaac remained quiet. Tabitha's eyes met his across the table.

"You look much better this morning," she said, hopefully loud enough so he could hear.

"I wish I could say the same about you." He didn't smile, but she knew Isaac was teasing her—a good sign. She missed their friendship. At one time they were best friends, but that was before they'd grown apart.

Throat sore, Tabitha struggled to eat, the fork in her hand shaking. Before long, everyone had finished their meal.

Mr. Girod stood. "On behalf of our whole family, we want to thank you all for taking us in like this. And John, for giving me the shirt off his own back. But most of all for Tabitha, who risked her own life to save ours. For that, we are eternally grateful." His eyes were red.

It was the nicest thing Mr. Girod had ever said to her. He was a hard man, not giving credit often.

"It was the Lord who saved you all. I was only His helper. And you are more than friends to us. You're our family. I'm so glad God has brought us all back together." The emotion of the moment made her tremble from head to foot.

Mama stood. "We'd better get her to bed. Frieda, can I get Isaac to help?"

"*Nay*," Tabitha said. "He can't." Tabitha gave Isaac one more glance before she weakly stood on shaking knees and started for the stairs. "I'll be fine."

Rosanna and Mama were at her side in an instant.

"FRIEDA, your soup is *sehr gut*. You'll have to teach me how to make it." After sleeping a few more hours Tabitha was able to sit up in bed and talk as she ate.

"I save it back for when someone is sick. I've got a bunch of it in the cellar. Luckily, we still have our canned foods."

Tabitha's mind drifted back to the night before, remembering Frieda's anger at her husband. In the light of day, Frieda was in good spirits again, her brown eyes soft and *mueterly*.

"I'm sorry about the house, Frieda. It's a shame to lose everything you worked so hard for."

Frieda sat on the edge of the bed beside Tabitha. "I have my life and the lives of my whole family, thanks to you and God. I have nothing else to wish for." She smiled confidently.

Tabitha hoped she would be that strong if such a hardship fell on her family. "Still, it's difficult. I wish I could help more. I feel bad having you wait on me, bringing me food all the way upstairs."

Frieda laughed. "You've become a fine woman, Tabitha Hilty. How is it you're not married yet?"

Tabitha felt the heat rising to her cheeks. "Just waiting for the right someone, I guess."

Frieda's smile faded. "That's something I wanted to ask you about. Roy has seen the looks you and Isaac exchange. He thinks you're courting. I know it's none of my business, but if you are, I'd like to know before he does. He's not going to take it well, having a courting couple living in the same house."

"*Nay.*" Tabitha looked down at the soup bowl in her hands. "We courted once though. Over a year ago. It didn't work out." Tabitha frowned at the memory.

"Was he..."

She raised her eyes to meet Frieda's. "He was nothing less than a perfect gentleman. You brought him up well." She set the bowl on the side table. "I don't know. Being childhood friends may have prevented us from ever being more." Tabitha shook her head slightly. "I'm still waiting for a spark.

Maybe that's silly, though. I just wish Isaac and I could go back to the way it was before. Now he doesn't want to be my friend at all, and to tell you the truth, I miss his friendship." Tabitha stared longingly at her empty hands where they rested in her lap.

"Well, I appreciate your honesty. I'll tell my husband he has nothing to worry about and as for you... Well, you're going to make some man very happy one day. I have no doubt about that." Frieda felt Tabitha's forehead just like *Mueter* would before she left the room.

WITHIN A FEW DAYS, Tabitha felt better and decided to join the rest of the house for breakfast downstairs. There were seventeen people living there now. The sight of the table was a bit overwhelming, knowing this was the new normal until the Girods finished rebuilding their house.

Frieda acknowledged Tabitha's presence first, her brown eyes growing big as Tabitha approached. "Feeling better?" she asked.

"Ja, danki." Tabitha sat down quickly, not wishing to be the center of attention. The table was full of food: a big platter of bacon, another with scrambled eggs, and even biscuits and gravy. Tabitha was hungry, but the overpowering smell of spicy meat threatened to send her back to her room.

Apparently, she'd missed the prayer as everyone was already digging in. Tabitha sat quietly, waiting for her stomach to settle again.

"Can I pass you something?" Isaac asked.

She looked up at him, his eyes oddly soft. "Just a biscuit, please."

He held out the plate of biscuits to her.

"Danki." A shirtless image of Isaac unconscious on the

17

floor assaulted her. She'd pulled with everything she had to get him out. She hoped at the very least he'd want to be friends again in return, but only time would tell.

"Are we working today?" she asked loudly.

"*Ja,*" Mama said. That was all the information she would get until after breakfast was over and she received orders from *Dawdie.*

Tabitha managed to get her biscuit down, the whole time aware of the glances Isaac sent. She wondered what they meant.

NORMALLY, the first five hours of the day were school-time for all the children under fourteen. Tabitha and Isaac's parents had pulled their children from the Swiss Amish school years ago to homeschool them, allowing them more time to work at the family business and pursue other interests. After breakfast, the table was cleared and dishes done, making room for children and their books.

Roy left for the Girod's place to care for the animals, but told *Vater* he'd return soon. Mama and Frieda would supervise both the children and *Vater's* aging parents while *Dawdie,* Tabitha, Rosanna, Isaac, and Joseph went to the cabinet shop to work.

"I don't want you spraying for a while," *Dawdie* said as they entered the dusty shop, the faint smell of varnish lending a strange comfort to her still-weak body.

"Why not?" Tabitha coughed.

"That's why. Rosanna will do all the spraying. Don't let Isaac or Joseph near it, either. You'll have to help me teach them how to make cabinets." *Vater* watched the young men cross the room.

"Surely they already know."

Vater laughed. "They're strong farm hands, and I'm sure they've built their share of buildings, but you'd be surprised at what we've learned about cabinet making over the years."

Tabitha thought. "We could give them piddly work." It was the name they used for the easy jobs they saved for Henry and Eli when they were interested in helping, things like putting on the knobs and handles or sorting screws. If they didn't want to help, Mark would do it. At twelve, he could do most anything in the shop with little supervision.

"*Nay*, they all want to earn their keep. The ground's too soft to rebuild their house just yet, and we don't know how long they'll be staying. This afternoon you'll have Mark, Henry, and Simon to help. I'll tell the women to keep Eli with the girls and see if they can keep them busy in the house and out of your hair."

"You're leaving?" she asked.

"*Ja*, after dinner when Roy gets back we're going out on an installation job."

It was up to Tabitha to keep the shop going. "Don't worry about a thing," she said with a smile.

Tabitha walked over to where Isaac and Joseph stood on the other side of the long shop table. "Hand me that tape measure," she said, ready to get back to work. She'd been sick long enough. Now it was time to earn her keep again. Joseph handed it to her and both of them leaned in to watch. "We need to pre-drill some holes to make sure they look clean when we're done, and it'll speed things up when *Dawdie* goes out to install them." She stretched the tape measure out, and with a quick mental calculation, grabbed the pencil from the table. After she had the wood piece marked, she looked up from her work to Isaac and Joseph. Joseph stood with his thumbs around his suspenders, and Isaac's hands were in his trouser pockets.

"Any questions so far?" she asked. Their eyes moved from Tabitha to the floor and then to each other.

"What is it?" she asked quietly.

Isaac shuffled his feet, then he extended his hand to her. *"Danki,"* he said, his eyes filled with regret as his gaze met hers. Tabitha's breath caught at the touching gesture. She clasped his hand and shook it. Heavy and roughened from calluses, his touch was warm and electrifying.

The Girods were taught not to touch a woman outside of their own family for any reason other than a handshake, beginning when they completed their school studies at about thirteen. As Tabitha let go, she remembered the last time she'd touched his hand.

It was summer. They had just finished the eighth grade at the Amish school before their parents decided to home-school instead. All the children were playing in the field between the two houses next to the creek. Isaac had both of Tabitha's hands, spinning her as fast as his feet could turn him.

"I'm dizzy." She laughed, the warm sunshine heating her *kapp.* Her feet lifted from the ground as he spun her faster, the air around her forcing her body up.

"Hold on tight," he yelled as his straw hat sailed off his head.

"Don't let me go, Isaac," she squealed. It was just like him to do something ornery like spinning her till she was sick, then letting her fall hard to the ground.

He didn't.

When he stopped, she stumbled into his arms, knocking them both off balance. She landed on top of him in a heap on the ground, both laughing. She'd never forget his radiant face at that moment or the happiness they'd shared. It was the last time she'd touched him until the night of the fire.

"You saved our lives," Isaac said, bringing her back to the present.

"*Ja,*" Joseph said, "We wouldn't even be here if it weren't for you." He extended his hand, too.

Tabitha shook his hand. "You two are like my own brothers." The words were unexpectedly difficult to speak. She looked down at the cabinet piece, rather than meeting their eyes, blinking rapidly. "I know we haven't been close in years, but...I've never forgotten." She wiped her eyes with the backs of her hands.

"Well," she said, trying to lighten the mood, "I'm glad to be working with you two again. There aren't many frolics where men and women work together." She smiled and handed Isaac the tape measure. "You can mark the ones on that side. They're all straight across from these." He took it from her carefully, his hazel eyes searching hers deeply.

Joseph coughed a little, then a lot. Tabitha handed him a cough drop from her dress pocket. "You're not getting sick, too, are you?" she asked.

He unwrapped the cough drop and popped it in his mouth, shaking his head. Isaac spoke for him. "It's the smoke. Some of it's still in his lungs."

"I'm so sorry, Joseph," Tabitha said. "Do they know what started the fire?"

Isaac looked at Joseph, whose breathing didn't sound as labored.

"I had a lantern lit, waiting for Isaac to get home from the singing. I remember him coming in and we talked a little bit." He shook his head, his voice strained. "I don't remember after that. I guess I left it lit and kicked it over in my sleep."

"Is that how you remember it?" Tabitha asked Isaac.

"I remember he had the lantern lit when I came in, *ja*. He never should have had it going." Isaac marked the wood with a pencil.

"I know. I was a *doomkupf*. Believe me, I'll never forget it." He coughed some more. "We were just lucky you didn't go to bed as early as Isaac, or we'd both be goners."

Tabitha cleared her throat uncomfortably.

Isaac peeked up from his work. "She must have been entertaining someone in that fancy parlor of hers," he whispered casually.

So they'd heard about her parlor. "It's not fancy," Tabitha said. "And for your information, it's a perfectly respectable courting practice. I light a candle and place it in a holder. When the candle gets down to the rim, my company has to leave."

"I've seen courting candles before," Joseph said. "You can make them last a few minutes or hours, depending on how you set them in the holder." He glanced at his brother. "Lucky for us, she liked this guy."

Tabitha's face burned. *Dawdie* was giving her a questioning look from across the shop. She was glad they were teasing her, though. It was almost like old times, but *Dawdie* was depending on her to get the work done and she wouldn't let him down.

"All right," she said with a smile. "Enough chit-chat. Back to work."

Isaac smiled but didn't look up.

A while later, the shop door opened and *Gruszmawmie* and *Gruszdawdie* walked in, arm in arm, *Gruszdawdie* walking with his cane in his other hand.

Tabitha dropped the tape measure to the table with a clank and ran to them. "May I help you?" She refrained from calling them by name, unsure what mental state *Gruszmawmie* was in. *Gruszdawdie* was never in the same world as the rest of them, but she had only begun to fade in and out.

"We're in *Rumspringa* and would like a room," *Gruszdawdie* said in a small, feeble voice. It wasn't often he spoke anymore. Tabitha vaguely remembered a joke he used to tell about wanting a room while in *Rumspringa* but she couldn't remember the punchline.

"I think I can help you," she said. "Follow me." She held the door open and led them back into the house. When she ushered them inside, she called out, "Mama, you've had a jailbreak."

Mama appeared quickly with a dish towel in her hands. "Oh, Land's sake! Where were they?"

"They came into the shop."

She threw the dish towel over her shoulder and took *Gruszdawdie's* arm. "Sorry, Tabitha. I think Eli left the door unlocked. He finished his work early and went out to check on Chippy. I should have been watching closer." She shook her head.

"It's okay, Mama. You've got your hands full. Is it almost dinnertime?"

"About an hour. Frieda and I are working on it now."

Tabitha nodded before returning to the shop. Inside, she found Rosanna had caught up on the varnish spraying and was batting her eyes at Joseph. She guessed Rosanna didn't see Joseph like a brother. Tabitha clenched her jaw.

Isaac leaned over the worktable. "I hadn't seen your grandparents do anything at all since I've been here. I figured they sat in their chairs all day."

"Well, occasionally one of them gets a wild hair and takes off," Tabitha said.

"Do they ever talk sense?" he asked.

"*Gruszmawmie* usually does, but not as much lately. If you want to talk to *Gruszdawdie,* just mention horses, hat-brim widths, or haircuts." Those were the usual h's most Amish men liked to talk or argue about, and *Gruszdawdie* was no exception.

Isaac laughed. "I may try that sometime."

It was good to see Isaac laugh. It dissolved the uneasiness Tabitha felt around him, making her forget exactly why they had broken ties in the first place.

Before long, Frieda was at the door announcing that dinner was "being took up." Tabitha had always wondered why the expression wasn't "being put down" but had never asked.

When Tabitha entered the house, *Gruszdawdie* was bent over, looking under his kitchen chair.

"What's he doing?" Isaac asked Tabitha as they sat down at the table.

"Don't ask," Tabitha said.

"Leora!" *Gruszdawdie* snapped. "What'd you do with my suspenders?"

Gruszmawmie cupped her hand up to her ear and said, "What?"

"My suspenders! You hid them again, didn't you?"

Mama took his arm and guided him to sit in his chair. "We'll help you look for them after dinner."

Nose scrunched up, Tabitha whispered across the table to Isaac, "He usually forgets by then."

The silent prayer dragged on a little too long for *Gruszmawmie*. Before *Dawdie* shuffled his feet to indicate prayer time was over, she was snoring loudly in her chair. Isaac met Tabitha's eyes as their heads rose. Tabitha placed her hands in her lap and looked away, waiting for the food to be passed to her.

After dinner, Tabitha put the young boys to work under Mark's supervision. Then she found something for Rosanna to do that wouldn't allow her to make eyes at Joseph. Just to be sure, she gave Joseph work facing the opposite direction. There wasn't much left for Isaac and her to do except sand. They each stood on one side of the workbench with a block of sandpaper, smoothing out the rough edges of the cabinet doors.

"You've learned a trade most men haven't, do you know that?" he said, watching her skilled hands.

She scrubbed at the wood faster. "Well, it's not forever, I hope."

"So you'd rather keep house?" His voice grew warm.

She smiled at his question. "*Ja*. I don't know a woman my age who wouldn't."

"Huh," he said.

Tabitha sensed a hint of agitation with the utterance. Her mouth drooped into a frown. And the day had been going so well. "Is there something wrong with that?" she asked.

"*Nay,*" he said in a tight voice.

Her eyes darted around the wood cabinet piece. "Maybe we should talk about something else." The scratching of sandpaper on wood filled the gap in their conversation.

Finally, Isaac spoke. "It's almost Christmas."

Tabitha smiled again. "Do you remember the Christmas when we were eleven and went caroling in the wagon?"

He nodded his head.

Tabitha laughed. "You pushed me out of the wagon before it got stopped and your *vater* almost threw you in the creek."

He glanced at her and then back down. "I didn't push you. You tripped."

Her mouth dropped open at his blatant lie. "I did not!"

"You're remembering incorrectly. I would never hurt you," he said, sounding more serious by the end of his statement.

Tabitha began sanding again, frowning. "I never said you did it on purpose." The dust in the air made her cough. She stopped, pulling a cough drop from her pocket. She placed it in her mouth then offered one to Isaac. Her hand touched his in the exchange.

"You did that on purpose," he said, scrunching his eyebrows together.

Tabitha smiled coyly. "You'll never know, will you?" She began sanding again.

"There's a good reason to remain hands-off during the courtship years," he said.

"And there's a good reason to hand over a cough drop without getting out the tweezers. It's called practicality."

"It's Biblical, Tabitha."

"And how will you ever find the girl for you? By asking her a bunch of questions?" She glanced at the others in the room and then lowered her voice. "What if she answers them all right, but when you finally kiss her it's repulsive? What will you do then?" she teased.

"You're just going on. The feelings you get for a person can be misleading. I personally like being in control of myself, so I don't make a bad decision, like marrying someone I'm not compatible with."

Tabitha pushed her cough drop into her cheek and swallowed hard. "Well, I'm glad we found out early that we weren't compatible." Tabitha walked away to check on the others in the shop, the whole time, sensing Isaac's eyes following her around the room.

CHAPTER 3

*I*saac's family had always had family Bible reading and devotions after supper dishes were washed. The Hilty family had always done it after breakfast. The two families decided to combine and have them together in the evening. Mr. Girod would stand with his family Bible open in one hand and command, "Bonnets to one side, suspenders to the other."

The girls would sit on the floor against the wall in the living room and the boys would form a line facing them a few feet away. This left a strip of space between them wide enough for Mr. Girod to pace back and forth as he spoke, looking much like Bishop Amos on a church Sunday. *Dawdie* would stand on the other side with his Bible, checking references.

The discussion topic posed for the night was where Cain had gone wrong.

"He killed his brother," Henry answered simply.

"*Ja,*" Mr. Girod said, "but what about before that?"

"He offered the wrong offering?" Joseph asked.

"But why?" His *vater's* eyes twinkled.

Isaac's forehead wrinkled in deep thought. "Because he did it with the wrong heart."

"*Nay*," he said.

Dawdie cocked his head. "What do you mean, *nay?*"

"*Nay*, there was something before that." Mr. Girod paced quietly. "Does anybody know?"

"Sin was crouching at his door." Rosanna squirmed and repositioned her legs.

"*Ja*, but why?"

Tabitha spoke. "He didn't do well because his countenance had fallen." It was the only thing in the verse left unguessed.

"Exactly." Mr. Girod pointed to her, looking very excited.

"What's that supposed to mean?" *Dawdie* snapped.

"Well," Mr. Girod began, "your countenance is the expression on your face. If you walk around with a sad face all the time, can you do anybody any good?"

Dawdie shut his Bible with a huff. "You can't mean he committed the first murder simply because of the look on his face."

"How do you take it?" Mr. Girod asked.

"You can't take every verse that literally, Roy."

"Why can't you? It makes sense to me."

Tabitha shut her Bible the same time Isaac closed his. He smiled at their similar actions. It was obvious the "study" was finished. Now they would remain seated until both their *vaters* decided to call it a night. Sometimes Mr. Girod could bring out things in the Bible that made the whole group think. Other times he seemed to argue for the sake of arguing. Tabitha wondered how hard it must be to live under his authority. Perhaps it was why Isaac was so stuck in his ways.

She noticed Isaac eyeing her. Her heart fluttered in

response, but she looked away. They couldn't talk until Bible study was officially dismissed, but he was saying something with his eyes. Maybe he was sorry for the harsh words they'd spoken earlier.

THE NEXT MORNING AT BREAKFAST, Eli entered with a squirrel on his shoulder.

"Oh, no you don't!" Mama said, her hands planted firmly to her hips. "No squirrels at the breakfast table."

"Oh, Mama, Chippy won't hurt nobody."

"Don't backtalk your *mueter*," *Dawdie* said as Eli headed out the door.

It usually took a few minutes for all of them to get settled at the table, but the silence was beginning to get awkward as they waited for Eli to wash his hands. But it gave Tabitha time to reflect on the fact that Isaac no longer stared at her every time they were in each other's presence. As glad as she was to get out from beneath his intense scrutiny, she found she missed his stares. Everyone was quiet except the two youngest girls who were whispering to each other.

Finally, *Gruszmawmie* looked around and said in a loud, gruff voice, "Who died?"

Isaac smiled behind his clasped hands, his elbows propped up on the table.

"No one, *Gruszmawmie*," Tabitha said with a timid smile. She had the seat closest to her.

"Then why does everyone look so grim?"

A twinkle entered *Dawdie's* eye. "Perhaps their countenance has fallen."

Tabitha shook her head, a slow smile slid across her face.

After breakfast, Ruth Schwartz stopped by to deliver two

half-bolts of fabric. It was a wonderful gift. Frieda fingered the dark blue cloth longingly.

"I imagine you're tired of wearing our clothes, aren't you?" Tabitha said.

"*Ja*. But it was still very kind of you."

"If you'll get started on cutting out the pieces, I can help you sew them after work today," Tabitha said.

Frieda shook her head tightly. "Oh, no, dear. You work hard enough the way it is."

"I don't mind a bit. But it'd be even more fun if you'd let me sew for Isaac. He'd hate it that I touched his clothes so much." A laugh bubbled up before she could help herself.

Frieda bit her smiling bottom lip. "Don't mention it to my husband and you've got yourself a deal." She laughed. "It's good to see you two are at least talking again."

"Well, perhaps we'll never see eye-to-eye, but I certainly have missed having him around. I'll see you at dinner?"

Frieda nodded and Tabitha exited the house, ready for another hard day's work.

SATURDAY CAME and there was no work in the shop. It was a catch-up day to finish everything else around the house that had been neglected since the Girod family had moved in. Isaac and Joseph walked over to the remains of their old house to do some clean-up while everyone else except Tabitha, Rosanna, *Gruszmawmie*, and *Gruszdawdie* had gone into town for groceries and supplies.

"The house is so quiet it's almost eerie," Rosanna commented. She sat in the living room, keeping a watchful eye on *Gruszmawmie* and *Gruszdawdie*.

"*Ja*, I keep wondering if everyone is asleep," Tabitha said wearily. It had been a long, hard week, and Tabitha craved a nap.

"Where's my suspenders, woman?" *Gruszdawdie* yelled.

Tabitha jumped. She blew out a lungful of air. "Well, almost everyone," she said to Rosanna before directing her next comment to her grandmother. "*Gruszmawmie*, did you ever take his suspenders?" she asked.

"What?" she yelled.

Tabitha drew closer to her ear and repeated her question slowly and clearly.

Gruszmawmie's face softened with a mischievous grin. "*Ja.* Every time he told a lie, I'd swipe 'em up and hide 'em. Once in the barn, and another time I dug a hole and put 'em down in it. Buried 'em." She chortled, seemingly proud of her actions.

"What did he lie about?" Tabitha asked.

"Oh, stupid stuff like when I caught him lookin' at Ruby Schwartz and he said he didn't. Taught 'im a lesson, it did." Her wrinkled skin, evidence of many long years. Years Tabitha sometimes wondered about.

"I'm surprised at you, *Gruszmawmie.* The Bible says to forgive, not to repay evil for evil."

"Well, how else was he to learn?" she asked in her serious, yet comical way.

Tabitha and Rosanna both covered their mouths, trying hard not to laugh at her grave expression.

Suddenly, *Gruszmawmie* said, "Who died?" and neither of them could hold it in any longer.

Just then, Isaac and Joseph came into the house covered with soot and mud.

"What's so funny?" Isaac asked.

"Well, not you two," Tabitha said, taking a good look at them both. "Get on outside and I'll find you both some clothes." At least they'd removed their boots at the door.

Washday was two days away and already almost every article of clothing in the house was dirty. She pulled out the only shirt and trousers left from *Dawdie's* drawer and then found the stack of clothes Frieda had been sewing. They usually took baths after dark, when it was easier to be discreet, but under these circumstances, it had to be done.

She opened the door. "I'll get you two some wash-water in the corner of the kitchen and we'll stay in the living room while you wash and change. It's all I know to do. But you'd better hurry before everyone else returns or it's not my fault who sees your backsides. I'm going to need help, though."

Isaac walked inside and followed her down the hallway and into another room where they kept the big tub. "You get that end," she said. It was then she realized she'd got him to break one of the rules—he was in a room alone with her.

He took one end and together they carried the tub into the corner of the kitchen, the only place it wouldn't be visible from the living room.

"Danki," Isaac said as he watched Tabitha fill the tub partway with both cold water from the hand pump at the sink and hot water from the reservoir on the back of the cookstove.

"You're welcome," she said.

He stood between her and the only way out of the room. Isaac paused, staring intently into her eyes.

"Your clothes are on the counter," she said quietly.

Isaac stepped out of the way, letting her pass, her heart pounding. She walked out of the room, suddenly feeling guilty for breaking his rules. Surely there had been another way. She should have had Isaac and Joseph carry the tub. What would it have hurt for the men to fetch their own water?

Tabitha shook her head. They were silly rules anyway. Not at all practical. Fetching water was no more romantic than handing a person a cough drop. Still, it nagged her as she considered the way she'd felt back in the kitchen.

Tabitha smiled when Isaac and Joseph re-entered the living room, clean and changed. "That looks nice on you," she said to Isaac, pointing at his shirt.

"*Ja*, this one actually fits," he said.

"That set is yours. Your *mueter* cut it out and I did the sewing."

"You did?" He looked down at himself.

"I did."

"Well," Joseph said, "I wish someone would sew me a set. I've got to roll up the sleeves *and* the legs."

"Sorry, Joseph," Tabitha said. "I'd get on it right now but I have laundry to do. Four men can't share clothes all week and make it to wash-day, I'm afraid. Someone will need to stay inside with *Gruszmawmie* and *Gruszdawdie* and someone else can help me with the wash."

It was meant as a joke. She figured the men could handle being alone with her grandparents for a little while, until everyone else returned home, but she didn't expect both Joseph and Rosanna to volunteer to stay inside.

Tabitha raised her eyebrows. "Well, I guess you three can figure it out. I'm going to go start the laundry."

She hauled the two large wash tubs outside and started to pump water from the outside hydrant.

Isaac suddenly appeared at her side. "What do you need me to do?" he asked.

"Can you build a fire under that tub?" she asked. "I'll go get the dirty clothes and the soap." She hurried into the house to gather them, and the fire was going strong when she returned. Usually, she'd wait for the water to get good and warm but the sun would be sinking soon, maybe before she finished, and the darker it got, the colder the air grew.

She threw a few of Mama's dresses into the water first.

They were the least dirty and she wanted to make sure Mama and Frieda had clean clothes to wear. Some of the water splashed her face.

Tabitha wiped at it with her dress sleeve. "You really don't have to help. I can probably get it all hung out myself before dark."

"Did you really make me these clothes?" he asked, pinching at the fabric on his leg.

"Ja."

"Mama always said a woman was serious when she asked for help, even if it sounded like she wasn't. You do so much work around here, it wouldn't be right to leave you with my laundry."

"Well, we're out here alone." She raised one eyebrow.

"Sometimes you have to be…practical."

"All right," she said with a smile. "I'll wash them and you can run them through the wringer." Tabitha watched as Isaac cranked a dress through, looking like it was the first time he'd even seen a wringer, much less used one. "You've changed a lot, Isaac."

"For the better, I hope."

"Ja," she said.

Isaac grinned. "I was hoping you'd say that."

Tabitha rubbed another dress up and down the washboard, plunging it into the water and out again. Then she squeezed the water out of it and handed it to him. Their hands made contact as he received it, and he dropped it in the water. "You did that on purpose," he said, suddenly serious again.

Tabitha was taken aback by the accusation. "I did no such thing."

"I thought you were different, Tabitha. I thought you respected me."

Tabitha shook the water off her hands forcefully and then

pushed her fists onto her hips. "This," she said, nodding toward the washtub, "this is why it didn't work out between us. I'd almost forgotten."

She watched him open his mouth to say more but the sound of the buggy made them both pause to look down the lane. Then Isaac shook his head and stormed off, entering the house through the kitchen door.

CHAPTER 4

*T*he Christmas cards had begun arriving, some for each family. They were all hung on a long string across the living room wall. Tabitha was sure it was the change of decor that made the children even more energetic than usual.

Eli had Chippy the squirrel in the house again, urging Isaac to pet him.

"Go on," he said. "He won't hurt you." Eli set Chippy down on Isaac's lap. Isaac looked up at Tabitha as if pleading for her to intervene.

She shrugged.

Isaac held his hand out in front of the squirrel and slowly started for his head. All at once, Chippy bit him on the finger and Isaac pulled his hand back with a yelp. The squirrel hopped away and Eli ran after it.

"He always was a good judge of character," Tabitha mumbled and turned down the hall.

As Tabitha exited the room, she wondered if there was a quiet corner for her to find a moment of peace. It was evening, supper was finished and everyone was waiting for Mr. Girod and *Dawdie* to come in and lead them in Bible devotions.

On her way down the hall, Tabitha discovered *Gruszmawmie's* door was open.

"I thought you were in the kitchen with *Gruszdawdie*," Tabitha said.

"What?" she asked.

Tabitha entered and sat down on the bed next to her. In her hands were a pair of *Gruszdawdie's* good suspenders. Tabitha chose her words carefully. "Tell me about courting *Gruszdawdie*."

The old woman's face lit up inside the brim of her *kapp*. "You know that bridge that lets you cross the creek?" she asked.

Tabitha nodded. She knew it well. They used it a lot to get to the Girod's place.

"Marlin asked me to marry him on that very bridge. Well," she shrugged, "I was on the bridge. He was under it."

Tabitha was intrigued. "What do you mean, *Gruszmawmie*?"

She laughed. "I told him I was going to marry Atlee Miller and he dropped to his knees and begged me not to. Said I'd never be happy if I did." She sighed. "Then he got down in the middle of Swan Creek out there and said he loved me. He'd never said it before that. It was what I was waitin' so long to hear."

Tabitha held her hand to her chest. "Then what?"

"I told him to get out of the crick and go get the *Schteecklimann*. Back then, you had to have a *Schteecklimann* to do your askin' for you."

Tabitha had heard of the old tradition before. The duty was usually performed by a deacon—a sort of reenactment of the story of Isaac in the Bible, where Isaac's servant went to find his bride for him, but Tabitha figured it had more to do with the church approving the match than honoring biblical heritage.

"Well, what did the *Schteecklimann* say about poor Atlee Miller?"

Gruszmawmie leaned in close and whispered, "Not a thing." She smiled big. "Atlee Miller hadn't wanted to marry me at all. He was after Bertha Schwartz." Laughter bubbled up her throat.

"*Gruszmawmie*, you are an ornery one." Tabitha smiled. She wondered how the woman could have been so sneaky and still been blessed with a husband all these years and a big family. Tabitha certainly wasn't about to tempt God and try any of her shenanigans.

"Every year after that, Marlin would stand in the middle of Swan Creek and tell me he loved me." *Gruszmawmie* looked down at the suspenders in her hands.

"Are you planning on hiding those?" Tabitha asked with a raised brow.

"*Nay*, dear. I thought it might shut him up if I gave 'em back." *Gruszmawmie* stood and shuffled out the bedroom door.

Ornery or not, it certainly was romantic. Tabitha wondered if she'd ever find a man who'd love her like that.

Stepping into the hallway, Tabitha collided with Hannah. "What's your hurry?" Tabitha asked, catching the girl by her thin arms.

"I'm supposed to find you. It's time for Bible devotions. *Dawdie* said."

"Well, we'd better get in there, then." Tabitha took the young girl by the hand and led her into the living room where all the children sat in two neat rows. Tabitha sat down at the end with Hannah next to her. Across from them sat Joseph, who was making eyes at Rosanna.

Don't they know everyone can see what they're doing? Suddenly Tabitha was embarrassed for her sister, shaking her head as she lowered it.

Roy Girod began reading Ecclesiastes chapter three. "'To every thing there is a season, and a time to every purpose under the heaven: A time to be born, and a time to die; a time to plant, and a time to pluck up that which is planted; A time to kill, and a time to heal; a time to break down, and a time to build up.'" The words were moving enough, but Mr. Girod spoke with added feeling tonight. "'A time to weep, and a time to laugh; a time to mourn, and a time to dance.'" He stopped and, looking at Isaac, said, "Read the next verse aloud, son."

Isaac stood to his feet with his Bible in hand and scanned the page. "'A time to cast away stones, and a time to gather stones together; a time to embrace, and a time to refrain from embracing.'"

"And what do you think that verse means?" Mr. Girod asked.

Isaac looked up. "Just what it says, *Vater.*"

"That's right. You may sit." He caught Tabitha's eye before he turned on his heel in his pacing.

Tabitha had read the passage before, but never considered it carefully. So maybe the Girod way was Biblical at its core, but wasn't he still taking the verse a little too far?

IT WASN'T OFTEN they had a day off work at the cabinet shop. A frolic had been organized to clean up the Girod place. Since the two houses were so close, it made sense to do the cooking at the Hilty house and take it next door, rather than trying to cook outside, as they often did when they needed to work without a kitchen.

The children played in the yard with the many other children who had accompanied their parents. Fifteen buggies had brought the neighbors, according to Eli who was constantly running in and out with his squirrel on his shoulder. Rosanna sat with *Gruszmawmie* and *Gruszdawdie,* and Tabitha and the other women from the frolic were cooking in the kitchen.

"Mama, tell me about courting *Dawdie,*" Tabitha said as they peeled potatoes over a white five-gallon bucket placed between them at their feet. They sat facing each other in kitchen chairs, dropping the freshly peeled potatoes into a bowl of water on the table as they finished with them.

"What do you mean?" Mama asked.

"Well, *Gruszmawmie* said she and *Gruszdawdie* had a *Schteecklimann* when they courted. I know you two didn't have one. So what was it like to court back then?"

Frieda laughed but put her hand over her mouth when Mama looked up at her. Mama raised her eyebrows. "Do you want to explain it?" There was an unspoken warning in her voice.

Frieda shook her head, smiling. "*Nay,* she's your daughter."

Tabitha watched as Frieda tugged on Tabitha's oldest sister Sarah's dress sleeve from behind and thumbed at Mama.

Mama blushed as a small audience gathered. She lowered her voice as she spoke. "Back when your *vater* and I courted we followed a practice called bundling."

Frieda tapped Mama on the shoulder with the back of her hand. "Go on," she prodded, the side of her mouth turning up slowly.

Mama smiled bashfully. "A young gentleman would come to your house after dark—"

"At bedtime," Frieda added with a single nod.

"At bedtime, and your *mueter* would bundle the both of you up in sacks and covers—separately of course," she said, pointing a finger in Tabitha's direction. "Then a long board would be placed between the two of you in the bed."

"The bed?" Tabitha's eyes widened.

Mama spoke slowly. "*Ja*, and then the lantern was blown out."

"In the dark?" Her eyes grew even wider.

Sarah began laughing and Frieda stomped her foot on the floor.

Mama continued, "*Ja*, in the dark. My *mueter* had a rhyme. Since in a bed a man and maid, may bundle and be chaste, it does no good to burn out wood, 'tis just a needless waste.'"

Tabitha's mouth dropped open. "You're not kidding, are you?"

"*Nay*," Mama said, and began peeling the potato in her hand again.

"How long did they do that?"

She shrugged one shoulder. "The next morning someone would unbundle them and he'd go home."

"*Nay*, Mama, I mean, how long did the practice continue?"

Frieda's eyebrows rose. "I've heard some still do it. The bishop says it was the smartest thing the devil did since he put the serpent in the garden."

Mama pressed her lips together. "The practice evolved into church singings after dark and after-hours parlor visits by candlelight. But even those are falling out of fashion."

"As they should." Frieda shook her finger at Tabitha.

"But you have to understand," Mama said, "even back

then, they weren't encouraging couples to be naughty. Everyone was still supposed to behave."

"And did they?" Sarah asked.

"Not all of them. But your *vater* and I did. You were made proper," Mama said, looking at Sarah.

Sarah's whole face twisted. "Oh, Mama, that's more than I needed to hear."

The potato slipped from Mama's hand and into the peeling bucket, and she covered her face, laughing. Soon the whole room filled with uncontrollable laughter. Even Rosanna peeked in to see what was the matter. A frolic with the women of the community was much better than working in the woodshop with the men—indeed.

A FEW DAYS LATER, *Gruszdawdie* sat in the living room asleep with his good suspenders wrapped tightly around his arm. Tabitha figured he was afraid *Gruszmawmie* would steal them away from him if he set them down. The woman was ornery enough.

Tabitha looked around the room. Nightly devotions would start soon, but something didn't feel right. Where was Rosanna? Tabitha stepped outside the kitchen door and crossed the yard. It was nearly dark.

A new outhouse had been constructed to help accommodate all seventeen of them. The original was a double-seater, the one on the left side was for the women-folk, and the men used the one on the right, but it did nothing to prevent long lines of people waiting their turn. Now they had two outhouses.

Tabitha drew nearer to the new outhouse, which was given over to the women. She heard a giggle but saw no one. Eyes narrowing, she entered the outhouse and locked it, then climbed up on the bench beside the seat, listening. The old outhouse had cracks between the boards, but not this one.

She stepped down and opened the door just enough for one eye to see out. Rosanna darted past, toward the house. Tabitha waited patiently. A moment later, Joseph strolled by with his hands in his trouser pockets.

AT THE NEXT SINGING, when Daniel Shetler held his hand out to help Tabitha into his buggy, she almost didn't take it. She could still hear Mr. Girod's words echoing in her ears.

"It is good for a man not to touch a woman. First Corinthians 7:1."

He'd been saying it a lot to his boys lately, but the way Tabitha always seemed to catch Rosanna and Joseph at the outhouse at the same time, she wondered if it had done any good.

As they drove the buggy down the road toward her house, Tabitha wondered if Isaac was taking anyone home. The man was stubborn—just like his *vater*. When he was right, he was very right, but when he was wrong, he'd never admit it. But either way, she was starting to think he was right about no-touch courtships. It was too easy to get lost in someone's hazel eyes and forget what a person was really like inside. It didn't matter, though. She was in control of herself, unlike her sister Rosanna.

"I had a real nice time tonight, Tabitha," Daniel said as they neared her house.

He was a nice man, but perhaps it was time to end it. The spark Tabitha was waiting for simply wasn't there for him. The only time she'd ever felt a spark in her life was when she'd touched Isaac, but if he was right, those were just fickle feelings, not love.

Would she ever find what she was looking for?

From the side of the yard, she spied the silhouette of a man.

Isaac?

She'd forgotten to tell him the doors would be locked. He'd never find his way in without her help.

She allowed Daniel to help her down from the buggy, standing a little closer to him than she was comfortable with. Her eyes darted back and forth between the two men, her breath shallow. "Would you like to come in for a visit in the parlor?" she asked finally.

Daniel's face lit up. "I'd like that."

Isaac met them halfway to the house. "The doors are all locked," he said.

She turned to Daniel. "Wait here while I unlock the door for you," she said timidly. Tabitha strode around the side of the house, Isaac following close behind.

"You're going to let him in?"

She was second-guessing the decision herself, but she wasn't about to reveal that to Isaac. "*Ja*, we're going to visit awhile in the parlor," she said without emotion. She stopped at her bedroom window and began removing the screen.

"In the dark? Alone? Do you really think that's a good idea, Tabitha?"

Tabitha pushed the screen inside and lifted her leg.

"What are you doing?" he asked.

"Trying to get inside." She grunted. "A gentleman would at least give me a leg-up."

"Get down from there," he said. "And put your leg down, I might see up your dress."

"Then stop looking!"

Isaac moaned. She felt his strong hands take hold of her waist, pulling her back down to the ground. Tabitha stood straight, her arms crossed, turning to face him. "Was that really necessary?" she whispered. He could get angry when the rules were accidentally broken, but then he would break them himself. Was there no rhyme or reason to his actions?

"You're telling me that's the only way in?" He eyed the window.

"*Ja*, we keep the doors locked so *Gruszdawdie* doesn't wander off in the night. I don't have a key. If you'd rather do it, go right ahead. You can unlock the door for me so I can let Daniel in."

"Daniel," he said mockingly.

"*Ja*. Daniel. Now hurry up, he's waiting." She glanced behind her, wondering what Daniel would think of the delay, and admonishing herself for her reckless behavior. She watched Isaac climb into her bedroom. "Take off your shoes, they're muddy!" she called. He turned around to face her at the window. "Just tell him to leave," Isaac said flatly.

"I will not. For your information, I rather enjoy his company."

"It's not right, Tabitha, and you know it."

She swallowed hard. "It's not for you to say."

He closed the window behind him. Tabitha slid it back open with a huff and climbed inside. She was surprised when she saw he was still there, facing her.

"Do you want me to kiss you? Is that it? Here, in your bedroom with our parents asleep down the hall?" His voice was an angry whisper. "Is that what would make you happy?"

Her breath caught at his reprimand, his words bringing instant heat to her face. *"Nay,"* she said quietly.

"If that's the kind of husband you want, maybe I should."

"It's…not what I want, Isaac," she whispered lowly.

"Could have fooled me."

She watched him walk out of the room.

Tabitha quickly replaced the screen and shut the window, her heart pounding in her ears. She made her way to the door and unlocked it, meeting Daniel outside. "I'm sorry, Daniel. I didn't mean to keep you waiting." She let him in and led him to the parlor.

She wondered what he would expect from her. The truth was, it was the first time she'd invited anyone in and she wasn't sure what would happen. With a slight tremor in her hands, she lit a candle and placed it deep into the holder. "We'll visit until the candle goes down to the rim." Her voice quivered.

"That sounds good to me."

Tabitha gestured to the pillow-lined bench and Daniel removed his hat as he sat down. She seated herself next to him, suddenly feeling confined. "Is it warm in here to you?" she asked, fanning herself with her hand.

"I was thinking the same thing," he said with that far-away look he got every time they neared her house in the buggy.

She inhaled a deep breath. "Uh, Daniel," she said, releasing the air from her lungs. "Tell me about yourself and uh...your plans for the future." She sat up straight, waiting for his answer, hoping it would be a long-winded one.

"I'm going to take over for my *vater*, you know that."

Tabitha's mind raced.

Horses, hat-brims, haircuts.

"I was thinking that the hat-brim requirements here are much different than in Gawson's Branch. Have you heard anything about that?" She glanced at the candle.

Daniel tilted his head. "Are you feeling all right?" he asked, scrunching up his nose.

"Nay," Tabitha said, planting her face into her palms. "I'm not. I'm sorry, Daniel. I shouldn't have invited you in. In fact, I don't think this is going to work between us at all."

He stood.

She wanted to explain further, but how could she? She wasn't sure of her feelings herself.

Tabitha watched Daniel's buggy drive away, wondering just what a godly courtship was supposed to be like, and why she'd done a foolhardy thing like inviting him into the parlor in the first place.

FINALLY, Tabitha had a moment alone with her sisters. Sarah, Liza, and Rosanna all sat on her bed. The neighbors had arrived again to help rebuild the Girod home, and that meant they'd need to start the noon meal soon.

A question battled inside Tabitha, but she wasn't sure how to bring it up. The conversation had gone from how to keep biscuits from burning on the bottom to the best kind of hairpins that didn't hurt when you removed them.

Sarah started to get up. "I guess I'd better go see if Mama needs some help."

"Wait," Tabitha said. "I need to ask a question. Without Mama."

Sarah sat back down, her eyes searching Tabitha's.

Tabitha's face grew warm. "What's it like…to kiss a man?"

"That depends," Sarah said carefully. "Are you courting someone?"

Rosanna got a big smile on her face. "It's like jumpin' in Swan Creek in mid-July, and all at once instead of wading in slow."

Sarah and Liza's eyes grew round. "How do you know?" they asked at the same time.

"I've done my share of kissing," she said, her nose in the air.

"With who?" Sarah asked.

Rosanna shook her head. "I'm not one to kiss and tell."

47

Sarah looked to Tabitha as if waiting for confirmation.

Tabitha cocked her head to the side. "The whole house knows who you've been kissing. That's why Mr. Girod is in such a hurry to finish his house—so he can prevent a wedding."

Rosanna's mouth dropped open. Her sisters laughed as she hurried out the door, slamming it behind her.

"Joseph?" Liza whispered.

Tabitha nodded. "If Mr. Girod does find out… Well, I pity poor Joseph."

Liza touched Tabitha's arm. "Don't worry about what Rosanna does, just be yourself."

"I know," Tabitha said. "But lately I've been listening to Mr. Girod and thinking maybe I'd like to save my first kiss for *after* I'm married."

"Well, what's wrong with that?" Sarah asked.

"You don't think it's silly?" Tabitha bit the side of her thumbnail.

"Nay," Liza said.

"But how can you be romantic without touching someone?"

Liza threw herself back onto the bed, staring up at the ceiling. "I remember the most romantic thing my husband ever did for me."

"What?" Tabitha asked.

"The dishes."

Sarah laughed.

"Nay," Liza said. "I'm not kidding. Once I wasn't feeling well and he was so tired when he came home, but he helped me cook supper and did all the dishes for me. It was the sweetest thing and I'll remember it always."

Tabitha looked at Sarah.

"It's true," Sarah said. "Once you get all the kissing out of the way during courtship, dishes are all you have left."

Liza hit Sarah with a pillow. "Well, Miss Smarty Pants, what's your most romantic moment?"

"Let me think." She touched her bottom lip. "When we were courting he used to write me the most romantic letters. He never sent them in the mail, he just gave them to me before we parted so I could read them later. I still have them." Sarah smiled dreamily.

"What about your first kiss?" Tabitha asked. "Wasn't that romantic at all?"

"Sure it was," Liza said. "But who wants to carry around the memory of kissing someone other than your husband?" She raised one eyebrow.

Tabitha pointed to them. "So…both of you?"

They nodded. Sarah said, "It's not worth it, Tabitha. Follow your heart. It sounds like it's leading you in the right direction."

Tabitha felt much better after the talk with her sisters. So what if Rosanna had experienced something she hadn't? Tabitha didn't know who she would marry, but she knew whoever he was, she wanted to wait for him.

AT DINNERTIME, all the food was moved to the Girod place by buggy. The barn was cleaned out and tables set up for the many who'd gathered to help. Tabitha watched as the men pushed and pulled the heavy beams. In only a few days, the Girods would have their new home, if the weather held. It was warmer than average for December, but in Missouri that could change quickly. Tabitha held her wrap tight, soaking up the bright sunshine they'd been missing for weeks.

Frieda tapped her husband's shoulder and he spun around. A quick word was said and then Frieda hurried back to the barn. Mr. Girod waved all the men in and soon everyone was gathered for prayer.

Mr. Girod thanked God for saving his family from the fire, and for sending out so many people to help. Then he blessed the food. Soon a line formed around the long tables. Being December, the barn was still half-full of hay, and people used the square bales as tables and chairs once they got a plate of food.

As Mr. Girod came through the line he caught Tabitha's eyes, the look he sent seemed filled with accusation. Thinking perhaps it was meant for someone else, she glanced over her shoulder. No one was there. She met his eyes again, and the scorn they held turned Tabitha's stomach. What could have made him so cross with her?

Once the meal concluded and they cleaned up, she took Frieda to the side. "I believe your husband's put out with me and I haven't the slightest idea why."

The corner of Frieda's mouth turned up. "He doesn't even know what he's put out about half the time. I wouldn't worry about it." She picked up a stack of dirty dishes and packed them in the wagon, leaving the tables for the next meal.

Tabitha wondered if the stress of building a new house had gotten to him.

Isaac caught her eye as he walked past. He looked as put out as his *vater*. Had Isaac told Mr. Girod about inviting Daniel into the parlor?

Tabitha's face flashed hot. It wasn't right for them to judge her. She hadn't gone against her parents' wishes and she hadn't behaved improperly. There was nothing to feel bad about, she told herself.

So why did she still feel so guilty?

GAS-POWERED LIGHTS WERE SET up a few minutes before sunset and it was dark when the men stopped working to eat supper in the barn. As soon as the sun went down, the air grew much colder, sending icy chills through Tabitha. They faced a long night of clean-up afterward, but they'd made good progress.

She wearily fixed a plate for herself and spying Isaac sitting in the barn, she decided to talk to him. Carefully she climbed the hay, the bales making an endless staircase to the top.

She sat down next to him. He ate his food quietly, never looking at her.

"I know why you're put out with me and you shouldn't be. But that's not why I wanted to speak with you. I want you to tell me what you said to your *vater* about me." She took a bite of potatoes.

"I don't know what you're talking about," he mumbled.

"Don't lie to me," she said. "He liked me just fine before, but after a day talking with the men, he doesn't. You tell me."

"Perhaps he saw you kissing Daniel in the parlor and lost all respect for you."

Tabitha's mouth dropped open. "I did no such thing, Isaac Girod! For your information, I've learned a lot from your *vater's* Bible studies and have decided to give up my parlor room for courting purposes. Rosanna's still not old enough to take it over yet, but I've decided you were right about being alone with a man."

"I was?" He coughed.

"You sound surprised."

She watched the bump in his throat move as he swallowed hard. "It just hurts me that you would purposefully smear my good name to your *vater*. I've grown to respect him, and now he must think the worst of me."

"I didn't say anything to *Vater* about you. He's been angry with me most of my life. You get used to it after a while." He took a bite of pie.

Tabitha huffed. She picked up her plate and started back down the hay bales.

"What'd I say?" he called after her, but she only shook her head. Every time she confronted him about anything he either denied it or lied. It was positively maddening.

CHAPTER 5

*T*abitha went to bed too tired to think about Mr. Girod and his disapproval of her. However, at the breakfast table, Mr. Girod continued to stare Tabitha down. This, in turn, led Tabitha to give Isaac the evil eye.

It must have created tension in the room for everyone because all at once *Gruszmawmie* yelled, "Who died?"

"No one, *Gruszmawmie*," Tabitha said loudly, in no mood for humor.

"It's a big community," she said. "*Someone* must've died."

Down the table, Joseph sent starry-eyed glances to Rosanna. Tabitha wondered how long it would last—not their relationship, since she knew it would probably end the second Joseph moved out, but how long before Mr. Girod discovered it. She wanted badly to tell Frieda, but Tabitha was no tattle-tale. They'd have to figure out what was happening on their own.

After breakfast, Tabitha found Rosanna watching *Gruszmawmie* and *Gruszdawdie* in the living room. She seemed to prefer it to kitchen duty, always volunteering for the chore.

"You and Joseph need to cool it," Tabitha said under her

breath, making sure *Gruszmawmie* couldn't hear. "You're embarrassing the whole family and you don't even know it." Tabitha shook her head.

"It's my life, not yours." Rosanna crossed her arms defiantly.

"If you care anything for Joseph you'll stop this. His *vater* won't take kindly to him disobeying, especially not at fifteen." Tabitha started to turn around, having spoken her mind.

"You're just jealous," Rosanna whispered.

Tabitha shook her head and marched into the kitchen before she said something she'd regret. She wondered what had made Rosanna stubborn and mean-spirited. They certainly hadn't been taught to be that way.

Stepping into the kitchen where the women congregated, Tabitha almost tripped over Eli, who was crawling across the floor. "What are you doing down there, Eli?" she asked.

"Aw, nothin'," he said a little too quickly.

"All right, out of the kitchen. Get your heavy coat on and go outside and play. I'm sure there are more children in the field by the creek."

"Do I have to?" he whined.

"*Ja,* we've got a lot of work to do in here. Unless…you want to do women's work with us." Tabitha raised her eyebrows at him.

"Nope!" he said, before jumping up and running out the door. He slammed it behind him, but then ran back in. "It's cold out there!" He grabbed his coat from the hook by the door.

Tabitha turned her attention to the food preparations already underway. A cheese tray was being assembled by Sarah. Two women sat with a bucket between them as they peeled potatoes, and the meat was already slow-cooking, so

Tabitha pulled the flour from the cabinet and began mixing a pie crust.

"Is Rosanna still in there with *Gruszdawdie* and *Gruszmawmie?*" Mama asked.

"*Ja.*"

"Well, I think it's high time she took a turn in the kitchen. Do you want to trade with her?"

"*Nay,* it's okay, Mama. I'd rather work in the kitchen." Tabitha dumped a cup of flour into the bowl. A small cloud of dust rose and Tabitha waved it away from her face.

Liza approached their *mueter.* "I'll trade with her a while, Mama. I need to get off my feet a bit anyway."

Tabitha and Mama had suspected Liza might have been with child, but it would be a while yet before Liza would confirm it to anyone. Rosanna ambled into the kitchen a moment later looking for something to do.

"You can finish up these pie crusts if you want and I'll start the filling," Tabitha offered. It was one of Rosanna's least favorite tasks. She said she could never get the crust right, and they'd fall apart when she transferred them to the pie plate. She hated mending them even more.

Rosanna frowned but didn't say a word. She stepped up to the bowl and began adding a little water while stirring with a fork, forming little balls of dough in the flour mixture.

As Tabitha reached for the shelf, she saw something flash in the corner of her eye. She snapped her head around. Chippy the squirrel was bounding across the floor. He made a chattering sound as he ran, leaping onto Rosanna's dress, and climbing up.

Rosanna screamed and Chippy landed in the flour bowl. With a flick of his tail a cloud of flour exploded in the air.

"Eli!" Mama shouted.

Tabitha caught the squirrel with both hands, holding him close to her. She tried to calm him down, holding him away from everyone. The poor thing was shaking. She dusted the flour from his tail and quickly handed him a little piece of cheese from the tray on the counter, his favorite treat.

Eli ran in and she passed him over, giving her brother a wide-eyed warning to go quietly and not return for a few hours. The other women stood with mouths gaped open.

Tabitha couldn't suppress her smile as Rosanna stormed off to the washroom, her black *kapp* coated with flour and her face covered in it.

Chippy always was a good judge of character.

BY DINNERTIME, the sun had hidden behind a mass of dark clouds and an occasional snowflake whipped in the wind. Tabitha huddled deep in the hay wall in the Girod's barn, trying to stay warm while she ate.

Isaac approached her, his straw hat in his hand. He sat down and a moment of silence passed before he spoke. "There were times when you made me waver in my convictions," he began.

She looked up from her chicken casserole questioningly.

"But now I'm firm in them. *'With my whole heart have I sought thee: O let me not wander from thy commandments.'* I hide that verse in my heart and turn to it often." Isaac sat quietly another moment. "I'm glad you've seen the truth with me."

Tabitha tilted her head to one side. "All of God's Word is the truth, don't you agree?"

He nodded his head. "I do."

"Then not bearing false witness against your neighbor is also an important commandment to follow."

Isaac blinked his eyes rapidly. "I didn't say anything to my *vater* about you and your *beau*." He let out a frustrated sigh, rolling his eyes as he shook his head.

Tabitha hesitated, but the look on his face was convincing. "I believe you," she said quietly. She stirred her pie filling with her fork. "And Daniel's not my *beau*. Not anymore."

Isaac grinned.

Tabitha saw the doors of friendship opening once again, at least she hoped it was. She missed her old friend dearly.

WHEN THE ROOF WAS FINISHED, the men stopped for the day. It wasn't quite dark yet, but the snow was looming overhead, ready to start any moment. If it wasn't much, they'd be able to work again tomorrow. Tabitha prayed for the clouds to move away while she fixed supper plates for both *Gruszdawdie* and *Gruszmawmie*. It was much too cold for them to be hanging out at the Girod's barn and who knew what kind of trouble they'd get into if someone wasn't watching them every second.

She covered both plates with foil and stacked them on top of each other, doing her best not to smash the pie. It was easier to walk with plates than to take the buggy.

The wind was cold and Tabitha was glad to have her leggings on under her dress. She stepped carefully over the footbridge and soon was in her yard. In the distance, a voice carried on the breeze.

Rosanna. Tabitha spied her sister and Joseph standing next to the horse stalls. Rosanna couldn't keep this up forever and not get caught. Tabitha took a deep breath as she passed by them.

In the house, Tabitha smiled at Liza and then handed the plates to *Gruszdawdie* and *Gruszmawmie*. "I hope you like it," Tabitha said loudly. She watched *Gruszdawdie* inspect it. "This is barn food," he said gruffly. "Who's gettin' a barn?"

"It's a house building, *Gruszdawdie*. Our neighbors, the Girods, are getting a house built."

"I built this house," he said. "Long time ago."

"I know, *Gruszdawdie*, and you did a fine job."

He looked at the food in his lap. "Barn food, huh? Who's gettin' a barn?"

"The Girods," *Gruszmawmie* yelled in his ear.

"I ain't deaf, woman!" he snapped.

"Oh, *bishstil* and eat your supper!"

Tabitha giggled to herself. It wasn't often you heard an Amish woman tell her husband to shut up.

"I can stay here, Liza, if you want to go eat now."

Liza shook her head slightly. "*Danki*, but I think I'll wait till I get home."

"You could go visit a while."

She smiled weakly, her head resting on the chair back. "I'm fine right here in this chair, but you need to be out where the men are."

Tabitha's face warmed as she turned to the door.

Outside, she spied Rosanna laughing. "Time to help clean up, Rosanna," Tabitha called to her. "If we get done quick we can have Bible study tonight."

Rosanna smiled at Joseph, and with a final look of what could have been reluctance, headed toward the Girod's.

Tabitha fixed herself a supper plate and sat down on a bale of hay. She spied Isaac heading in her direction on the other side of the barn, making her heart flutter in her chest. Then someone sat down beside her. She glanced at Levi Shetler, Daniel's cousin.

"Hi," he said.

"*Vie gatz*," she returned.

"It's going to be a real nice house, isn't it?" he asked.

Tabitha watched Isaac stop and turn the other way.

"*Ja*, it is."

"You know, Tabitha, I was wondering…"

Tabitha's mind raced.

Horses, hat-brims, haircuts.

Tabitha stood. "I have to go."

"But you haven't finished your supper." His lips parted as he rose to his feet.

"I know, but I just remembered something on the stove back at home. I'll see you later, Levi. It was *guete* talking to you."

She hurried off with her plate in her hand. Carrying it across the field, she wondered why she was suddenly so nervous talking to men. Reaching the footbridge, she sat down, dangling her feet above the rushing water. It was cold where she sat, but at least she could eat in peace.

She pierced her pumpkin pie with her fork and considered the situation. What was it she was waiting for? She knew she'd need to be straightforward when she courted, letting potential suitors know up front she intended to save all physical contact until after her wedding day. Still, she could have let Levi ask his question.

She began eating her pie.

"What are you doing out here?" Isaac asked.

Her heart pounded at the sight of him. "Having supper. You?"

"Out on the footbridge?"

"Are you going to tell me it's inappropriate for me to be alone with my supper on the footbridge?"

He laughed. "*Nay.* I suppose what a woman does with her food is between her and her plate."

Tabitha pressed her lips together in a slight smile.

"What did Levi want?"

"He wanted to court me, but what business is that of yours?" She took a big bite of pie and stared at the crust that remained.

"So do you have a new *beau* already?"

"*Nay*, not yet. I suppose you want a place in line with my suitors?" She raised an eyebrow at her plate.

"Well, the thought had crossed my mind." He sat down beside her, hanging his feet off the bridge. His boots almost touched the water.

She frowned. "We tried it once, Isaac, and it didn't work."

He reached his hands above his head, holding onto the rail. "Are you telling me you don't have feelings for me at all?" It was spoken matter-of-factly, but Tabitha could sense some hidden emotion in the question.

She spoke carefully, not wanting to hurt his feelings. "I do, but I think they're all the wrong ones."

He nodded and then slowly stood. She thought he was going to say something, but instead he walked away without another word.

THE WORDS ISAAC had spoken swam in Tabitha's mind the whole time she cleaned tables at the Girod's work frolic. Before long, the women were headed back to the house for Bible devotions before bed.

As Tabitha entered the living room she heard *Dawdie* telling Mr. Girod, "I have eight children, Roy. I can't watch them every minute. I do my best and let them learn from their own mistakes." He stopped talking when he saw Tabitha.

It sounded like they'd finally caught on to Rosanna and Joseph's sneaking around. It was about time.

She sat down with the girls in their row as Mr. Girod opened his Bible. "The Word teaches us that love is like a fire that, when started, can easily get out of hand, like the fire that destroyed our home. Many waters cannot quench it, nor can the floods drown it, it says. And the Bible also warns against stirring up love before its time." He paced back and forth as he spoke. "I believe someone here has awakened love before its proper time, and now that person will have to fight the flames. Can any of you imagine fighting the fire that took our home?"

Everyone shook their heads.

"Could it be done alone?" he asked them.

"Nay," they all said.

His voice rose. "Then come forth, ye workers of iniquity, and repent." Mr. Girod stopped walking and eyed Isaac.

Tabitha heard Isaac draw in a sharp breath. "I've done no wrong, Vater," he said.

Mr. Girod's fiery stare turned to Tabitha.

"Are you accusing me?" she asked.

Mr. Girod's eyes darted to the rest of them. "Off to bed, everyone. Except you two."

Tabitha watched as the others stumbled to their feet and rushed from the room.

"What's this about, Vater?" Isaac asked. Tabitha jumped to stand beside him.

Dawdie crossed his arms. "Roy saw you two leaving your bedroom late Sunday night."

Isaac's mouth dropped open. "I did nothing improper," he said.

"He's telling the truth." Tabitha's eyes pleaded with Dawdie.

Mr. Girod shut his Bible loudly. "Then you're calling me a liar."

Tabitha shook her head at her vater.

"Just tell the truth, Tabitha," Dawdie said, nodding.

"We're both telling the truth. Mr. Girod, you saw us both come out of my bedroom because after we came home from the singing the doors were all locked. My bedroom window is the only way in because *Dawdie* hasn't made me a key." She sent a pointed look at her *vater*.

Dawdie spoke up, "She's telling the truth. I can't find the keys anywhere, so I can't have one made."

Tabitha crossed her arms in front of her. "I've known Isaac my whole life and he's always been a gentleman."

Dawdie smiled. "See there, Roy? There was an explanation after all."

"So it seems," Mr. Girod said.

"Mr. Girod, do you believe I'm telling the truth?" Tabitha waited.

"*Ja*, I suppose you are," he said finally.

"*Guete*. I believe you owe us an apology, then."

His eyes narrowed. "Do you forget your place?"

"She's right," *Dawdie* said, a repressed smile forming on his lips. "There's nothing wrong with admitting fault. And you were wrong, Roy. Admit it."

He was caught. Mr. Girod cleared his throat loudly. "I apologize…to you both."

Tabitha smiled and held out her hand, and with a sudden look of curiosity, he shook it. "I want to thank you for leading the Bible studies these past few weeks. I've learned a lot from you." She turned to go, but then stopped. "And you're on the right track, Mr. Girod, only you've accused the wrong people."

"What do you mean, Tabitha?" *Dawdie* asked.

"Oh, you'll see soon enough."

CHAPTER 6

*T*he next morning before breakfast, Tabitha passed Isaac in the kitchen. She opened the refrigerator door and searched for leftovers from the day before.

"That was amazing the way you stood up to my *vater* last night."

She continued to dig. Under two half-eaten pies covered with tin foil, she found the cheese tray and pulled it out. "Nothing amazing about it. Truth is truth."

"Well, I still think it was pretty brave."

She took a piece of cheese and broke it into little bits, shoving them into her dress pocket.

"What are you doing?" he asked.

"Just bringing out the truth." She slid the tray back into the refrigerator and shut the door. "See you at breakfast." Tabitha grabbed her wrap and hurried out the kitchen door.

Outside, she sprinkled the bits of cheese behind the new outhouse, then found Eli playing in the yard. "Eli, may I borrow Chippy for a minute?"

"Sure, but why?" he asked, skipping toward her.

"I'm going to teach him a little trick."

63

"Oh, boy!" he said, handing over his beloved pet.

THE MEN SAT around the table making plans for the day and drinking coffee as they usually did in the morning while the family assembled. The women were cooking and the children playing, each running in and out of the house to do their individual chores. During that time, Tabitha kept her eyes on Rosanna and Joseph. Soon she saw Rosanna leave the house and two minutes later Joseph followed. Then she motioned for Eli to bring in Chippy.

Eli poked his head inside the door. "Mr. Girod, come outside. Tabitha has taught Chippy a trick. You have to come see!"

"A trick?" *Dawdie* said. "I'll be right there." He often played along with Eli.

He stepped inside. "Sure, *Dawdie*. Come quick." Eli ran out the door and everyone followed. Eli gave the squirrel to Tabitha who set him down on the ground. They watched him take off, bounding through the yard as if he'd been shot at.

"Not much of a trick," Henry said. "I've seen him run lots of times."

They watched as the squirrel disappeared behind the outhouse. Then they heard a scream.

Tabitha hid her smile behind her hand. Earlier, she had shown Chippy some cheese she hid there and knew he'd run back to it once he had the chance. When Chippy saw Rosanna he wouldn't be able to resist jumping on her, as he always did. Something about Rosanna was annoying, even to a critter like Chippy.

As expected, Rosanna ran into view, stomping and squealing as the squirrel climbed her back. Joseph's arms flailed trying to get it off her.

Mr. Girod's face reddened while snorting like an infuriated bull. He started yelling and waving his arms.

Tabitha hurried into the house, not willing to see what happened next. She hung her wrap on the hook and sat down for breakfast. It would probably be a while before anyone ate. The food was ready, but the people weren't.

Soon, Isaac sat down at his place across from her. "How did you know they were out there?" Astonishment filled his hazel eyes.

"Please don't tell me this is the first you're learning of it," she said quietly.

"*Nay*. I warned Joseph but he wouldn't listen. You were right, they had to be stopped."

Tabitha could hear yelling from both their *vaters* now. "What do you think will happen to them?"

He leaned back in his chair. "I don't know, but I think they deserve it."

Gruszmawmie came in, her arm linked with *Gruszdawdie's*. She shuffled her feet across the floor and stopped him at his place at the table, before releasing him. They both sat down, *Gruszdawdie's* cane between them. She looked at Tabitha, sounding out of breath when she asked, "Who died?"

THE SNOW STARTED FALLING hard as the buggies arrived. Mr. Girod sent all the volunteers home, afraid the roads might get too bad for them.

Soon it would be Christmas and no one would work at anything for a few days while they visited with family. *Dawdie* had decided to get things caught up in the shop, especially since they would be making cabinets for the new house soon.

Joseph, who claimed he never touched Rosanna, was sent to

work shoveling out the horse stalls for both families while his *vater* supervised. Rosanna worked in the shop. They each had to eat alone in separate rooms during breakfast. Tabitha figured they wouldn't get any more chances to be alone together. Now she understood why youth their age were kept from attending joint frolics, to prevent the mixing of very young singles. Keeping them separate until courting age had been an effective way to protect them from lighting a fire they couldn't contain.

Tabitha measured the cabinet frame with the tape measure, marking the wood with a pencil. Then she slid the tape measure across the table to Isaac who stood on the other side.

"Why don't you want to be with me?" he asked quietly. His expression grave.

Tabitha glanced around. Rosanna was spraying cabinet doors and *Dawdie* was working the saw. When she glanced back at him, Isaac's eyes pleaded for an answer.

Her heart pounded. "This isn't a conversation for the shop," she said.

Just then, *Mueter* appeared from behind the half-open door. "I need Rosanna to watch your parents for a bit," she said to *Dawdie* who had stopped working the second she entered. "Frieda is out with Roy at the new house. There's no way I can keep up with them and the children, and start dinner. I can have her back in half an hour. Will that work?"

"Nay," Vater said. "She's being punished. Take Tabitha."

"Mr. Hilty," Isaac said. "I need to speak with your daughter. Would you mind if we both went? Just for a few minutes?"

Vater gave him a quick up and down then glanced at Tabitha. She nodded her consent.

"All right. But I need both of you back here working in half an hour if we're going to get anything done today."

Isaac followed Tabitha next door and into the living room. Most of the children were at the long table in the kitchen doing school work while *Mueter* flitted to and fro. Chippy ran past and so did Eli, nearly tripping Tabitha.

Gruszmawmie and *Gruszdawdie* sat in the living room holding hands. *Gruszdawdie* had his pair of good suspenders wrapped tightly around his cane, propped up beside them. Tabitha covered her mouth at the sight. She glanced at Isaac to see if he noticed.

"That's very...forward," he whispered.

"I think they forget we're here sometimes," Tabitha said, smiling. "I think it's romantic."

"I was hoping we could discuss our own romance," he said.

She walked to the far corner of the room and Isaac followed. "What romance?" she asked.

"Well, there could be one," he said with a slight smile forming.

"I don't know, Isaac." Tabitha shook her head.

"What's there to know?"

"It didn't work last time, what makes you think it will work now?" she asked.

His hazel eyes danced around her face. She had to admit, she wished with all her heart it could work, but knew it never would.

"We're different now. You understand me better and you can finally respect the way I believe."

"What?" Tabitha's forehead tightened.

He moved closer, his arms crossed. "You wanted someone who would sweep you off your feet, a man who would kiss you first and ask questions later. But now you know that's wrong, Tabitha."

She put her fist to her hip, her head tilting to one side.

"You think the reason we broke ties was because you wouldn't kiss me?"

His eyes darted around her face again. "Well, wasn't it?"

"Nay! I ended it because you could never admit when you were wrong and, apparently, it runs in the family. And there's nothing wrong with wanting romance. Look at *Gruszmawmie* and *Gruszdawdie*."

Tabitha turned in their direction. Shock bolted through her. The chairs were empty.

Her eyes shot around the room. The door stood wide open. Her eyes met Isaac's in a tense exchange. They both lunged for the door, then looked outside in all directions, but neither one could be seen.

"Get the others. All of them," Tabitha said, her voice laced with panic. Then she ran out, not waiting for his answer.

She sped around the side of the house. The snow was beginning to blanket the frozen ground. Tabitha sprinted around the corner. Across the yard by the footbridge, she spotted them.

Not the creek!

Gruszmawmie stood on the bridge with *Gruszdawdie*. Then, *Gruszdawdie* crossed the bridge.

Where is he going?

Her heart in her throat, Tabitha ran hard in their direction.

Gruszdawdie stepped closer to the water, plunging his cane in first. All at once she knew what they were doing.

He's going to propose.

Tabitha reached the creek, kicked off her shoes, and jumped in. The icy water shocked her system. She drew in a quick breath. Quickly, she swam across as *Gruszdawdie* waded out to meet her. He stumbled on the steep embankment, catching himself before he fell.

"No, *Gruszdawdie*! Go back," she said. The cold water

pricked at her like needles. She caught him as he stumbled again. His cane washed down the creek.

"I love you, Leora Hilty," he called to his wife on the bridge.

"Get out of the water, *Gruszdawdie*, you'll freeze." Tabitha tried to get him to turn around, pushing against his shoulder, but the rocks beneath her were slick and he wouldn't budge.

Suddenly, the sound of heavy boots clomping across the footbridge vibrated above her head. Tabitha's breath whooshed from her lungs as Isaac pulled at *Gruszdawdie's* suspenders, leading him out of the water. Mama had *Gruszmawmie* by the arm, and she and Rosanna led her off the footbridge.

Tabitha stood waist-deep in the cold water. She tried to climb the steep bank, but slipped on a patch of ice, sending her plunging into the water again and floating downstream. She swam toward the bank. Isaac leaned down, grabbed her by the hand and pulled her arm. Hard. Her feet slipped on the embankment's greasy slope. When she made it to the top, Isaac fell onto his backside, pulling Tabitha directly on top of him.

"Oh, that's cold," he said, wincing.

Tabitha's nose nearly touched his, they were so close. Water dripped from her face to his as she took in heavy breaths.

Tabitha rolled over, freeing him. She tried to stand but stumbled. Isaac picked her up in his arms, her teeth chattering, still dripping with near-freezing water.

"I'm okay," she said, but he made no attempt to set her down, carrying her boldly across the footbridge with her family watching.

"I…I…th-think I can walk," she said, hoping he wouldn't let her down.

"You're not even wearing shoes," Isaac said as he plodded along.

She buried her face in his neck, clinging to his warmth. His touch, like the flame of a candle, ignited something deep within.

He set her down when he reached the kitchen and Mama led her into *Dawdie's* room. Together they managed to strip her of her wet clothes and Mama threw a blanket over her to warm her up. "I'll go get you some dry clothes."

Soon she was dressed and, with a blanket wrapped around her shoulders, she entered the living room. *Gruszdawdie* had changed as well.

"How is he?" she asked, still shivering.

"He's fine," Mama said.

"Oh, Mama, I'm so sorry. It was all my fault." Tears ran down Tabitha's face. "I should have been watching better."

Mr. and Mrs. Girod entered the room, Hannah following.

"The important thing is everyone is okay," *Dawdie* said.

"What happened?" Frieda asked.

Tabitha looked at *Gruszdawdie*. *Gruszmawmie* threw her arms around him and kissed him on the mouth.

"Land's sake!" Frieda said, covering Hannah's eyes.

"I almost let *Gruszmawmie* and *Gruszdawdie* drown in Swan Creek," Tabitha said, still not believing what had happened. She sniffled.

"No, Tabitha," Mama said, "you saved them. Do you know how many times I've almost let them get hurt? Too many to count, but they have lives, too. Just look at them."

Mama hugged Tabitha from the side.

Isaac had changed clothes by the time he joined them a few minutes later. It looked like the set Tabitha had sewn for him. He stood with an uneasy look on his face. Perhaps he was upset at how close they had been. The memory brought warmth to Tabitha's cheeks.

His eyes darted from her to his parents and back again. "The fire was my fault," he said. "I let Joseph take the blame because he couldn't remember. It was his lantern, but he fell asleep first. It was my responsibility to put it out, but I fell asleep, too. I'm sorry." His reddened eyes threatened tears, and Tabitha wondered if Mr. Girod had taught his boys not to cry for any reason.

He'd held onto that fact all this time? What a heavy burden to carry.

She waited for his family to say something—anything—but they didn't. Her heart broke for him even more. She took the blanket off her shoulders and handed it to Mama, then walked over to where he stood. She extended her right hand to him and covered her mouth with the other. New tears began to fall as she shook his hand. His mama hugged him. Simon did as well. Then his younger sisters. The whole time Isaac's eyes never left Tabitha.

Finally, Mr. Girod shook his hand, pulling him in close. "We forgive you, son."

Tabitha wondered how many nights Isaac had laid awake, longing for those few words, but had been too afraid to ask.

CHAPTER 7

*E*ach of the adults took a cup of coffee with them to the shop, the pressing rush to get everything done now absent. *Dawdie* sang Christmas carols as he worked, and Tabitha and Isaac went back to marking and drilling holes.

"Danki," she said, as he stretched out the tape measure.

His eyes didn't leave the work table. "As I recall, someone pulled me from a burning building. I owed you one."

Tabitha took in the sight of Isaac in his new clothes, his hazel eyes downcast as he appeared to be absorbed by his task. His attention wasn't on her as it usually was when they worked, and she was surprised at the feeling of jealousy that came from it.

She remembered how he'd confessed to his family and how hard that must have been for him. It had given her a whole new respect for him.

"Well, I appreciate it all the same. I'll never forget it." She meant that. It was the most romantic thing anyone had ever done for her.

Isaac glanced up at her and then back down at his work. A half smile formed on his lips, lighting up his face.

THE DAY BEFORE CHRISTMAS, the women cooked and baked, making pies, cakes, and loads of candy. The men worked together in the shop, while the children enjoyed a day off from their schoolwork. Joseph and Rosanna both repented. Tabitha supposed it was because they didn't want to miss out on the fun of the holiday.

When Christmas came the mood was bright and wonderful in the Hilty home. Each person received a gift. Dinner was light, but when suppertime arrived, there was a bounty of delicious foods, some that were saved for once a year, like *Mueter's* cheesy casserole and Frieda's chocolate mint pie.

The candles were lit in the windows, and another set was placed at the center of each table. *Dawdie* said the prayer out loud, for it was a most special day of thankfulness, and when he was finished, everyone said, "Amen."

Tabitha looked around the table at the faces of the Girod family, knowing they would leave when their house was finished. She would miss every one of them. Hannah and Ada, who often needed Tabitha's help to get their hair brushed out and pinned up in the mornings before breakfast, and Simon who fit right in with her own brothers, Mark and Henry.

Then there was Joseph, who despite his faults was a good, hard-working boy. And Isaac, the hazel-eyed young man who had become her friend once again. She would miss him the most.

"Are you up for a game after supper?" Isaac asked.

Tabitha realized she had been staring in his direction. "What's that?"

"We could play a board game in the living room. Since we

don't have to work tomorrow we could stay up a while, if you wanted." He took a bite of mint pie.

"I'd like that," she said.

After supper dishes and all the chores were done, Tabitha brought in a thick blanket and laid it out in the corner of the living room. Isaac had a game of dice called Tenzi and a notepad and pen. They set the lantern between them and stretched out on the soft blanket. The trick was to get all of your colored dice the same number the fastest, but only using one hand to do it.

They made up other variations as they went along, to make it more challenging. Finally, they each took one die and rolled it at the same time to see who could get the highest number. They repeated the move so quickly that soon Tabitha couldn't remember who was winning.

"It'll be so quiet when your house gets built and your family leaves," she said.

Isaac held his die. "It might just be peaceful around here."

"I was thinking more like…lonely." She set hers down on the blanket.

He looked at the die in his hand, turning it over and over with his thumb. "Doesn't have to be."

Tabitha thought. It was tempting. He'd changed a lot, but still, she wondered if she could trust him. "The Christmas when we were eleven—"

"I pushed you out of the wagon," he said flatly, still looking down at the die in his hand.

She smiled at his honesty.

"I didn't mean for you to fall out. I was just trying to get you to pay attention to me." His hazel eyes met hers, as if pleading for forgiveness.

"That's probably the most romantic thing you've ever said to me."

"What?" He frowned, rolling his eyes. "That's not romantic."

"Romance is different things to different people. To some, it's holding hands and kissing, and to others, it's dishes and letters."

"Dishes and letters? What books have you been reading?"

She laughed. "I don't have time to read anything but scripture."

He sighed. "Our family believes in no touching during courtship, but there is one exception."

"Handshakes?" she asked.

"Besides that." His eyes danced as he spoke. "One kiss. At the time of engagement."

"I didn't know that," Tabitha said.

"Lights out." *Dawdie* stood in the middle of the living room, giving the familiar nightly call. Children rushed around, blowing out all the candles that were in the windows. "Make sure you get them all," *Dawdie* said. "We don't want to have to build another house this winter."

"We're expecting a lot of company tomorrow," Tabitha said as she stood. "We'd better get some sleep." She picked up the game and the blanket. *"Goot nacht."*

"Good night, Tabitha." His eyes held hers one last time before she took up the lantern and hurried out of the room.

Tabitha spent much more time than she meant to that night, wondering what it would be like to kiss Isaac.

THE DAY after Christmas was even more fun with all the extended family coming together, only this year there were two families. The house was filled to overflowing and Tabitha hadn't seen Isaac all day. She stepped outside, the warm sunshine a surprise. She almost didn't need her wrap.

The weather in Missouri changed quickly from snow and mud to warm and dry.

She hoped the weather held until the new house was completed, as Mr. Girod was beginning to get anxious about it, pacing back and forth any time it was brought up. She was sure he wanted to get Joseph as far away from Rosanna as he could, lest they be "tempted into more sin."

Tabitha found Isaac sitting alone on the footbridge, his hands in his coat pockets. She sat down beside him, dangling her feet over the side.

"I was hoping you'd meet me here," he said.

She smiled. "I suppose you have a question to ask me?"

He pulled his hands out of his pockets and wiped them on the front of his trousers. "Is there some reason I shouldn't?"

Tabitha took a deep breath. "I'll marry you, but I won't kiss you. Not till after we're married. It may be your tradition, but it's not mine."

She had thought long and hard about it. How often a couple would kiss and then break up, and Tabitha thought it may be possible kissing was the cause. Maybe they'd stirred up love before its time and couldn't handle the feelings it brought with it. Maybe because those feelings weren't meant for unmarried people. Tabitha wanted no part of that. Her first kiss would be with her husband and she'd carry the memory of it with her forever, unashamed.

Isaac smiled. "I'm surprised at you. In a good way," he added quickly. "I'm glad this isn't something I've pushed on you, but your belief as well. That's how you know it'll work."

"Well, I have one other condition."

"What's that?" he asked.

"You must promise you'll never lie to me again."

His eyebrows slanted. "I swear it. Only truth will come from my lips as long as we both shall live."

Tabitha smiled. "Then marry me."

He scrunched his eyebrows together tight. "Did you just ask me to marry you?"

"I'm sorry. That's not how it's supposed to go, is it?" Her cheeks felt hot.

"*Ja*, I'll marry you, Tabitha Hilty. I love you and there's nothing I want more than the chance to be a good husband to you."

"Your *vater* won't like it, that we're a courting couple living in the same house."

"I think we skipped the courting stage. I'll go tell him right away, and your parents, too, if you'd like. It wouldn't be right to hide it. With the re-building going on, we might have to wait a while to marry—maybe months." He looked deep in her eyes, saying nothing for a long while. "I'd always imagined this moment ending in a kiss."

Her cheeks burned. "I had, too. For a while, I felt cheated. Like I was missing out on something the other women had, but now I know what's really important. And I've had my romance. The way you carried me inside the house after pulling me from the creek was enough romance to last me a lifetime."

Isaac shook his head. "That's not romance. It was a necessity."

She laughed. "You can call it what you want, but I call it romance."

"I don't know," he said, a note of skepticism in his voice.

"Would you rather write me a letter?" she asked, knowing he hated writing letters.

"*Nay.*"

She laughed again. "I think we should visit with the families while they're here. It'll soon be suppertime and then they'll be leaving."

"Maybe you could meet me in the living room for a game again tonight before lights out?"

"Maybe." Tabitha gave him a playful look before she got up and walked back to the house.

Tabitha floated into the kitchen where her Mama sat with her married sisters. She smiled dreamily.

"Someone's sure happy today," Sarah said with a slight upturn of her lips.

Tabitha shut her mouth tight but the smile remained.

"You look like you're ready to burst," Liza said. "What is it?"

"I'm getting married," Tabitha said quietly.

Sarah let out a little scream.

"To who?" Liza asked.

"*Ja*, to who?" Mama's face was blank.

"Frieda's Isaac," Tabitha said, looking right at Frieda.

Frieda's mouth dropped open.

"I wasn't lying when you asked." Tabitha shook her head quickly. "We weren't courting—not since you've lived here with us. We courted about a year back," she said to all the women who had leaned in to hear. Mama stood up next to her.

"I believe you," Frieda said.

Tabitha relaxed a little. "We just decided…a moment ago. Isaac's telling the men, probably right now." She let out an anxious breath, her eyes opening wider at the thought.

Mama hugged her. "Congratulations!" she said.

"Do you think your husband will be happy for us?" she asked Frieda.

"I do. He told me not more than a week ago what a fine young woman you were."

Her sisters took turns hugging her as well, squealing with joy.

Finally, Frieda stood and hugged her close. "Now you're much more than a friend. Soon you'll be my daughter."

It had been a long day, but Tabitha met Isaac in the living room with the blanket and dice game after everyone had finished supper. He helped her spread the blanket, and they set the lantern in the center. Then they laid down on opposite sides of it and rolled the dice in the middle.

"I guess I forgot the notepad and pen," Tabitha said, getting lost in his hazel eyes.

"It doesn't matter if we keep score or not," he said, rolling a couple dice around in one hand. "I don't care if we even play. I just wanted to be near you."

"For how long?" she asked.

"All day." He smiled.

"I meant before that. We've been apart for at least a year. How long have you wanted us to be back together?"

He stared at the dice in his hand for a few moments. "You made me promise never to lie to you and I won't. But I don't really want to answer that."

Now her curiosity was piqued. "Why not? We're getting married soon, shouldn't we share everything?"

"*Ja,* but I don't want my *fro* thinking I'm a *doomkupf.*"

His woman.

The words sent a chill through Tabitha. "You'll never be a *dumb head,*" she whispered.

"When did you change your mind about me?" he asked.

She thought a moment, choosing her words carefully. "Last night when you admitted you pushed me out of the wagon. I didn't even have to ask. You knew I wanted the truth, even if it wasn't pretty. I knew then you'd changed. It was what I had waited for all along."

His eyes lit up. "You mean to tell me if I'd have admitted to pushing you out of the wagon, you'd have been my girl all this time?"

She nodded. "Probably."

"We could've been married already," he said.

"With *booplin*," she added.

"With *babies*…right," he said, shifting his body, his eyes wide.

She laughed hard at what they'd just said, her face hot. She couldn't believe she was discussing having babies with Isaac. Lands, how quickly things could change. He laughed, too.

"So," she said, when things quieted back down, "do you hope for a big family?"

"Nay," he said. "It's whatever the Lord gives, but I'd like to have a small family, maybe five *chinda* or so. You?"

"At least five," she said. "But more would be better. Do you have plans for where we'll live?"

"I don't know. We could buy our own place, somewhere in the settlement."

"Do you know the perfect place for a house?" she asked.

He shook his head.

"In the field across from the footbridge. It's beautiful and I've always loved that place. And it would be between both our parents' homes, just a stone's throw to either one."

"I doubt *Vater* will part with his good hay field, but I can ask."

"Would you? Oh, Isaac, that would be wonderful."

"I'm making no promises. He'll probably say no, but I'll ask."

"Well, then there's only the matter of when."

Isaac rolled the dice in his hand onto the blanket and then snatched them back up quickly. "We'll need to wait until things get settled around here with the new house. It wouldn't be fair to spring a wedding on everyone with everything else going on."

"You're right," she said. "At the rate it's going around here, it could be spring." She pressed her lips together tightly.

"We'll be married before spring, no matter what. I promise."

She admired the determination on his face. "I believe you."

CHAPTER 8

"*M*ama, come quick," Rosanna called from the downstairs bedroom. "It's *Gruszdawdie!*"

Tabitha had an uneasy feeling in her chest. She stepped into the room after Mama.

"Is he…" Rosanna's face was creased.

"He's gone," Mama said, touching his neck. "Go get your *vater.*"

Rosanna didn't move.

"I'll get him," Tabitha said. She ran through the house and found *Dawdie* sitting at the kitchen table with the men having their before-breakfast coffee. "Mama said to get you. It's *Gruszdawdie.*" She didn't have the heart to tell him what she already knew. With shaking hands, she poured herself a cup of coffee and sat down at the table, a knot forming in her stomach.

"What is it?" Isaac asked.

"He's gone home." It was the phrase they'd used so many times before to describe a loved one who was no longer living, but not in the Hilty house. Tabitha had never lost a family member before.

"I'm so sorry for your loss," Isaac said, glancing at his *vater* beside him.

She nodded slowly.

"Me, too," Mr. Girod said. He cleared his throat and stood to his feet, leaving them alone at the table.

She dropped her face into her hands, rubbing her eyes. "I keep thinking about what I did. Maybe if I hadn't let him get in the water—"

"*Nay*, Tabitha. You shouldn't think that way. It was an accident, and believe it or not, I think he knew what he was doing. Your *vater* told me how he used to jump in Swan Creek every year on their anniversary. He hadn't forgotten."

"He would have drowned if I had been any later."

"But he didn't. That's what's important. I almost killed my whole family in a house fire and I risked your life as well. They forgave me and I'm sure your *gruszdawdie* would forgive you, too."

Tabitha sighed, holding back tears. "*Viel dank.* You've made me feel a little better."

"You're welcome, and it's my job."

She wanted him to hold her and tell her it was going to be okay and somehow, without even laying a hand on her, he'd done just that.

Burial preparations took the place of the building frolic. No one would want to work on the house, thinking it might be seen as disrespectful to the family in mourning. Before noon, the community began bringing over food and offering to help with whatever needed to be done. Tabitha could see they were wasting the sunshine and she had nothing to do.

It hurt that *Gruszdawdie* was gone, but it hurt worse to look at *Gruszmawmie*, especially when she asked her favorite question. "Who died?" It was what she always said when the family wore sour expressions, but it also served to remind them that death was normal and nothing to be feared or mourned too long.

"I can't get *Gruszmawmie* to eat," Rosanna said. She'd been trying all day, but the woman refused. She didn't seem sick or even as heavy-hearted as the rest of the family was, she simply wouldn't eat.

"She's just being stubborn," Mama said. "She'll eat later."

When *Gruszmawmie* didn't eat supper that night, Tabitha knew. She loved *Gruszdawdie* with all her heart, even as ornery as she was, and she didn't want to be there without him.

Three days later they buried *Gruszdawdie*. That night *Gruszmawmie* went to sleep and didn't wake up.

THE SUN DIDN'T SHINE on the second of January, the day they buried *Gruszmawmie*. With Christmas over, everything looked dead and cold, all the excitement of the season gone and buried in the ground.

Rosanna sat in the living room in the spot where *Gruszmawmie* and *Gruszdawdie* usually spent most of the day.

"Are you okay?" Tabitha asked.

"It's hard to believe they're gone." Rosanna wore a blank stare. She had cared for them more than anyone else in the house. Tabitha had always thought it was to get out of doing other chores, but now, looking at Rosanna, she knew she'd been wrong.

Tabitha sat down next to her, and moved directly in front of her sister's face. Rosanna blinked and looked at her.

"They're happy now. Together. And *Gruszdawdie* won't

forget what's said anymore. I know it's sad, but we should be happy for them."

Rosanna nodded. "I know."

It wasn't often Tabitha had a moment alone with her sister, and there were things left unsaid. "I'm sorry about what happened with Joseph."

Rosanna huffed. "He lied to *Dawdie* and said he never touched me."

"Well, Joseph still has a lot of growing up to do, and you do, too. There's plenty of time for you two to be together... when you're older." Tabitha offered a smile.

"I'm never courting him again," Rosanna said. "Not as long as I live."

Tabitha laughed. "I think that's what I said about Isaac."

"Well, what changed?" Rosanna asked.

"He grew up. And in five years, I'll bet Joseph does, too. Then maybe you'll want to give him another chance."

Rosanna gave her a stern look.

"Or maybe not." Tabitha laughed, glad Rosanna wasn't upset with her anymore, and even more glad she had learned a lesson she wouldn't soon forget.

THE NEXT DAY, work continued on the Girod house. It wasn't customary to hold a frolic so soon after a loved one passed, but *Dawdie* insisted. They'd waited so long already and the weather was good. Word was sent out and the buggies began arriving.

Soon the women started coming in to prepare food for the noon meal. Rosanna tied on an apron.

Tabitha handed her a vegetable peeler. "You can be on potato duty today." She watched Rosanna sit down in a kitchen chair with a bucket at her feet and a bowl of water on the table beside her.

"Here, Mama, you can help her if you want," Tabitha said, handing Mama another peeler. It was one of the best jobs for sitting and talking, and it had been a while since they'd taken a turn together. She hoped it would lift Rosanna's spirits.

Tabitha was happy to be busy again. The days of not working had been so hard. She and Frieda began chopping onions for a special chili Frieda wanted to make.

Suddenly, Eli ran through.

Mama turned in her chair. "You'd better make sure your squirrel behaves himself today," she called.

"Yes'm," he said as he threw on his coat and ran out the door, not even shutting it all the way behind him. Sarah walked over and shut it properly.

Amid the onion-provoked tears, Frieda asked, "Have you and Isaac been making plans?"

Tabitha smiled at the thought. "A few. We still don't know where we'll live yet, but he says we should be married by spring, anyhow."

"Spring?" Frieda wiped her eyes on her apron and then continued. "Most couples marry in the fall or winter. Why would you wait that long?"

"Isaac said he didn't want to put anyone out with everything that's going to need to be done with the new house and all."

"Pish-posh," she said. "We'll be moved in a few days and in another week or two things will be just as they were. If you two are ready to be married, there's no reason we couldn't have a wedding together in...what do you say, Fern? Three or four weeks?"

Mama nodded. "Sounds reasonable."

Tabitha's heart skipped a beat at the news. "Oh, but it's really up to Isaac."

"I'll put a bug in his ear," Frieda said. "I'll let him know as soon as the house is built that there's no reason to hold off on our account. Why, you'll have a house of your own in the hayfield before you know it." She gave Tabitha a wink.

A tear streamed down Tabitha's face and she wondered if it was from joy or the onions. "Oh, *danki*. That would be wonderful."

TABITHA FOUND ISAAC AT DINNERTIME. She sat down next to him on a bale of hay with a plate of food. *"Vee bish do?"* she asked.

Isaac looked up from his pie. "Much better now that you're here beside me. How are you?"

"Fine, *danki*." She smiled at him. "It looks like there's a pretty good turnout today. There must be sixty buggies outside. I'm glad we cooked a lot of food."

"Ja, things are getting done, too. We'll be starting the inside later today."

Tabitha took a bite of potato. "We may have to take a day off then, to work on the cabinets in the shop."

He laughed. "Only you would see working in the shop as a day off."

"You didn't like working with me in the shop?" She was surprised. It seemed like he'd enjoyed it.

"I liked working with you, but I need to be outdoors."

"Even in the winter?" she asked.

"Even in winter. I like building, though. Maybe I could find work with a construction crew."

"With *Englishers?*"

"Ja, for a while. I know some men that do. We could share a driver."

Tabitha stared into his eyes, the flecks of brown and gold mesmerizing.

"I have something for you," he said. From his pocket came a small white square of folded paper.

"What is it?"

"It's a letter I wrote, but don't open it. Not here." He shook his head.

"That's so sweet, Isaac. *Danki.*"

"Don't thank me yet. I'm really no good with letters." He looked away bashfully. "It's just…I know you're the romantic sort."

"It doesn't matter. It's the thought that counts." She held the paper in the palm of her hand, her fingers closed tightly around it. "I'll treasure it always because it's from you."

He stood. "I guess we'd better get back to work. *Vater's* making every moment count today."

"See you at supper," Tabitha said. Isaac gave a tight smile and a nod before striding from the barn.

On the way home, Tabitha stopped on the footbridge and unfolded the letter.

Tabitha,

You asked me how long I'd known I wanted to be with you. The answer is always. You were my best friend growing up, and when Vater *saw us holding hands in the field when we were thirteen he forbade me to speak to you. I missed you so much over those years.*

When we were old enough to begin courting, you were always riding home with someone. I watched a new person come into your life every other Sunday, and I thought you'd forgotten me. I admit I was jealous and immature.

The time we courted was the best time of my life, but I took you for granted. You deserved so much better.

I promise to always honor and cherish you and to never let

selfishness or lies come between us again. Thank you for giving me
another chance.

> *Yours truly,*
> *Isaac*

Tabitha wiped her eyes on her coat sleeve and folded the letter. Her future husband loved her more than she'd realized. She longed for the day she could hold his hand again in the field by the footbridge.

ON THE FIFTH OF JANUARY, everyone pushed to get the work done. The next day was Old Christmas, a most holy and sacred day where no work would be done. They would fast until noon and then have a large meal together with family. This year, Old Christmas landed on Saturday, so the next day would also be a day of rest.

Everyone knew Mr. Girod was excited to celebrate Old Christmas in his own home. Tabitha wanted that as much as he did. The sooner the house was finished, the sooner a wedding could be planned.

Everyone worked hard all day, and by that evening the common rooms and half the bedrooms were ready. The Schwartz family brought over beds for everyone and a dining room table, and *Dawdie* installed the kitchen cabinets. The women planned to sew curtains the next chance they had.

Watching the Girods gather their things to move made Tabitha's heart ache, but she knew it was a sign of good things to come. The sun was setting as she stood with Isaac on the footbridge, the rest of his family already headed across the field.

"I'm going to miss you," she said.

He laughed. "I'll be right across the field if you need me."

She put her head down.

"I'll miss you, too," he said.

"I won't see you tomorrow, will I?"

"You could meet me on the footbridge after supper."

She smiled.

"And then there's church on Sunday."

"I guess you're right. I don't know why it feels like you're slipping away."

His eyes flashed concern. "Do you really feel that way?"

"*Ja,* but it's silly, I guess. You've made a promise and I know you'll come back for me soon."

He frowned. "I wish…"

"What?"

"I wish…I could kiss you right now."

Tabitha looked away. She wanted the same thing. Each time she looked into his eyes the thought crossed her mind, wondering what his lips would feel like to touch hers. But they had an agreement. Was he trying to get her to break it? She looked up, but Isaac had turned and was walking away.

"Where are you going?" she asked. Isaac didn't say a word. Had she tempted him further than he could stand? He pulled his boots off at the end of the footbridge.

"What are you doing?" she asked.

He flashed a reckless grin.

"Isaac?"

He jumped into the water with a "yip" and was suddenly standing waist-deep in Swan Creek. "Wow, that's cold!" he said, his voice high-pitched.

Tabitha's mouth dropped open. "Isaac, get out of there. You'll catch your death of cold."

"Tabitha Hilty," he said loudly. "I love you, and I promise to keep loving you till the day I die. Many waters cannot quench it, neither can the floods drown it."

Her heart swelled. "Okay," she said, smiling. "Now come out of there."

He climbed out and stood before her, dripping wet. Tabitha ran to him, reaching out, but stopped short of touching him. "You didn't have to do that, you know." She let out a heavy breath.

He slipped his feet back into his boots. "I know," he said. "But if your *gruszdawdie* could do it every year for no telling how many years, I can, too." His eyes danced over hers, teeth chattering loudly.

She stood close, embracing him with her eyes. "That was the most romantic thing I could ever think of." Then suddenly her heartfelt gaze gave way to laughter.

"What?" he asked.

Tabitha laughed harder, her hands covering her mouth. "*Gruszdawdie* and *Gruszmawmie's* anniversary was in the summer."

Isaac's whole body shook now.

Tabitha kissed her fingertips and then turned her palm outward. "Good night, Isaac."

"*Goot nacht,*" he said, and scurried toward the new house, his hands holding his arms close to his sides.

Tabitha laughed as she watched him cross the field, completely satisfied with her decision. Sarah and Liza were right. There were much more romantic things than kissing.

ABOUT THE AUTHOR

Tattie Maggard lives near Swan Creek, just south of a Swiss Amish community in rural Missouri. She enjoys singing in church, sewing and crafting, and writing short romances in her free time.

Sign up for Tattie's newsletter for updates and to get a free short story, Mending The Heart, sent straight to your inbox. Visit www.TattieMaggard.com for more info.

Thank you for reading and reviewing. God bless!

facebook.com/TattieMaggard

instagram.com/tattiemaggard

ALSO BY TATTIE MAGGARD

The Amish of Swan Creek

A Swiss Amish Christmas

Forbidden Amish Love

An Amish Rumspringa

The Amish Flower Shop

An Amish Heart

Amish Neighbors